Under the Shadow of Wings

SARA
HARRELL
BANKS

AN ANNE SCHWARTZ BOOK
Atheneum Books for Young Readers

Atheneum Books for Young Readers
An imprint of Simon & Schuster Children's Publishing Division
1230 Avenue of the Americas
New York, New York 10020

Book design by Nina Barnett

The text of this book is set in 13-point Sabon.

First Edition
Printed in the United States of America
10 9 8 7 6 5 4 3 2 1

Library of Congress Cataloging-in-Publication Data
Banks, Sara H., date.
Under the shadow of wings / Sara Harrell Banks.—1st ed.
p. cm.
"An Anne Schwartz book."
Summary: During 1944, life in rural Alabama brings changes
for eleven-year-old Tattnall as she realizes that she cannot always
protect her older, brain-damaged cousin.
ISBN 0-689-81207-8
[1. Cousins—Fiction. 2. Mentally handicapped—Fiction. 3. World War,
1939–1945—United States—Fiction. 4. Alabama—Fiction.] I. Title.
PZ7.B22635Un 1997
[Fic]—dc20 96-21180

Under the Shadow of Wings

For Christopher,
who records what's gone

Acknowledgments

No one writes a book alone. It is a creation fostered by who and what we've loved. I am indebted to those women who, by their loving kindness, nurtured and helped raise someone else's child.

I'd like to thank my editor, Anne Schwartz, who found the core of the book, and my agent, Ethan Ellenberg, for believing that it was there.

Sinners in the Hands of an Angry God was preached in 1741 by the Reverend Jonathan Edwards. Because it surpassed anything I might have imagined concerning the wages of sin, I used it as a guide for the revival sermon.

Then cherish pity, lest you drive an angel
from your door.
—William Blake, *Holy Thursday*

Under the Shadow of Wings

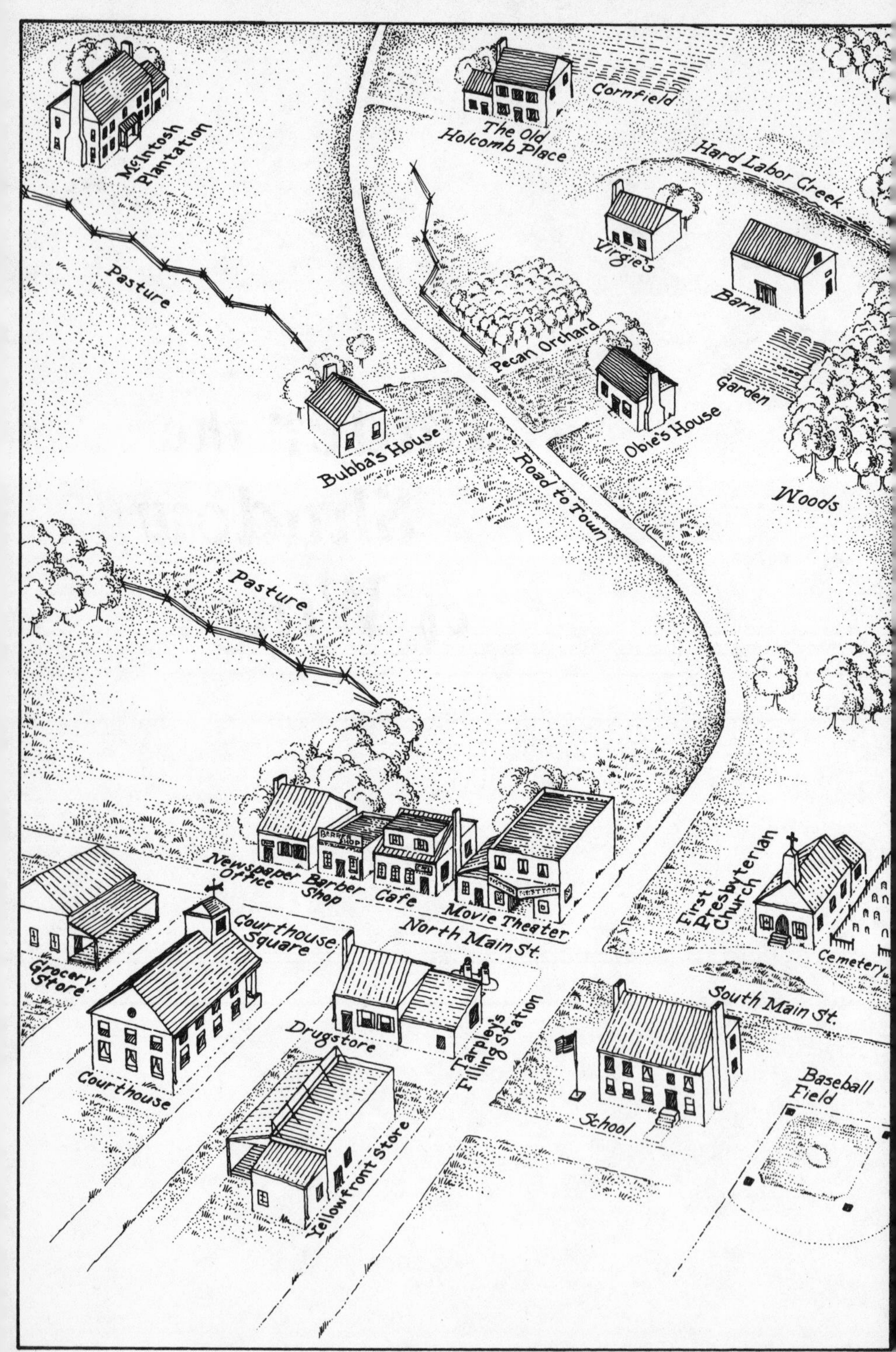

Map by Rick Britton

CHAPTER 1

Sometimes my cousin Obie thought he was a fire engine and other times he'd hold his arms out and buzz like an airplane. Everyplace he went. He almost never was a plain old person. Mostly he was something that went very, very fast. And in the end, it was as though he'd built up steam and was going faster and faster through his time until he'd used it all up. It took about a year till it was over, but he'd been working at it for fifteen. When it ended, and Obie Joyful was gone, he was sixteen and I was twelve.

I think it really began the day Obie, Bubba Tarpley, and I were flying kites out in the corn-field behind the house in March of last year. The wind was cold and blustery. My hair kept blowing in my eyes. I was sorry I hadn't worn a scarf like Virgie'd told me to, but it was too late. The dogs were hunting for rabbits through the broken cornstalks that littered the field. Obie's dog, Icarus, was a little bit faster than my dog, Lucky, but that's because Icarus had all of his legs.

"Yeeoowww!" Bubba yelled suddenly, running with his kite. He started up the rise, startling two rabbits, whose white scuts bounced like tennis balls.

"C'mon, Obie!" I called, following Bubba. The kites swayed in the wind, their long tails drifting back and forth, almost crossing from time to time.

Suddenly, there was a thrumming on the air like the hum of giant insects. Over the tops of the trees, six planes flew in formation, the bright shark faces painted on the fuselage of each clearly visible. It wasn't unusual for planes to fly over Pinella on their way to and from Maxwell Army Air Field in Montgomery. They'd been doing that for three years, ever since the war started in 1941. But we'd never seen planes like these before.

"Hoo, boy!" yelled Bubba over the noise of the engines. "Flying Tigers! Look, Tattnall, Obie! It's the Flying Tigers!"

Obie held his kite string with one hand and blocked the sun with the other. Bubba and I waved and yelled and ran after the planes until they were lost to sight. But Obie never moved. He watched those planes until they disappeared in the clouds and there was no sound save the wind soughing through the pines. He watched until his hands turned red and cold and his kite started to fall.

"Boy!" said Bubba, kicking at a dry cornstalk as he walked. "Would I like to fly one of *those* babies."

Then I remembered something. Something really good. "Hey, my daddy knows him!"

"Who?" Bubba asked, looking at me as if I'd just said a really weird thing.

"The man who started the Flying Tigers. You know, General Chen . . . something."

Bubba stood stock still. His kite dipped perilously. "You're makin' that up."

"No I'm not."

"You swear?" he asked. "Mr. Holcomb knows General Chennault?" He pronounced it *Shen-noit*.

"Cross my heart and hope to die. If you don't believe me, we'll go down to the paper and ask him."

Bubba hesitated for a minute. Not because he didn't believe me but I think more because he was surprised that anybody in our little town knew any heroes. Even though my daddy was editor of the paper and knew lots of folks.

"Aw, I'd sure like to talk to him, but I can't," said Bubba. "I've got to get home. My pa'll kill me if I'm late for supper again." He and I began to reel in our kites. Obie's was already down in the field.

"Tattnall," said Bubba, "do you realize that the general and his pilots practically fought the war in China by themselves? They're the most famous pilots in the world!" His nose was bright pink, as were the lobes of his ears that showed beneath his daddy's old brown felt hat.

I looked over at Obie, who was still standing in the same spot as when he'd first seen the planes. His army jacket hung loosely on his thin shoulders and his head was cocked slightly, as though he was still listening to the sound of the engines. He held his arms straight down and the twine of his kite string was tangled like a spider's web in the fingers of his right hand.

"Obie," I called, "it's about suppertime. Miss Clarissa'll be waitin' for you."

He looked at me like he'd been jolted awake. His tall, skinny body cast a long shadow in the setting sun. Handing my kite to Bubba, I walked over to him. I undid the string from his fingers and began rolling it back onto the stick.

"Here," I said, handing it to him. "Hold this while I button your jacket. It's gettin' cold. What happened to your scarf? You had it when we got here."

"Can I go home with you?" Obie asked as I retrieved the red scarf he'd wadded into a ball in his pocket.

"Bend down," I said, tying the scarf around his neck. "It's okay with me. Did you ask Miss Clarissa?" Miss Clarissa was Obie's mama and my daddy's sister. Which also meant she was my aunt, but I didn't claim her.

"I don't know," he said.

"You don't know if you can, or you don't know if you asked?" I said.

"I don't have to if I don't want to."

"Obie . . ."

"Obie," said Bubba, coming up behind us. "You're a riot."

Obie turned and punched Bubba lightly on his arm. "Yeah!" he said. "I'm a riot!" He flexed his skinny arms like a muscleman. "I'm a riot!"

Obie's real name was Obadiah, from the Bible. But since his last name was Joyful, his daddy had thought it grand to call him Obie. The story goes that during the War Between the States, the Confederates had a drink called "O.B. Joyful," which everybody in our family seemed to think was funny. That was why Obie's daddy named him that. But since Mr. Joyful was dead, nobody could prove it. He'd died when Obie was a baby, after being stung by a wasp in our grandmother's pecan orchard.

When Obie was about eight years old and I was four, I caught the measles and gave them to him. I got over them quick, but Obie didn't. Grandmother said that his fever got so high they had to pack him in ice to bring it down. The illness affected his brain and ever since he wasn't the same. When he walked, he threw his left foot out to the side, like it was stiff. And even though he got older, he still was like a little boy.

I think Miss Clarissa held me responsible for what happened to Obie. She never said so, but I could tell. I did my best to take care of him, since he wasn't always able to do it for himself. His eyes were weak, and he wasn't a very good reader, so I read to him. His favorite book was one with myths in it that our grandmother had given him. He loved the story of Icarus, whose father made him wings from the feathers of birds and taught him to fly. It's tragic, because Icarus flew too close to the sun and the wax holding the feathers together melted and he fell into the sea. But Obie just loved the part where Icarus soared high into the air. So when my daddy gave him a puppy one Christmas, Obie chose to name him Icarus.

Obie knew some other stuff too, like passages from the Bible. He did go to Sunday school every week, and sat in my class. He could name all the books of the Old Testament from Genesis to Malachi and didn't even get mixed up down near the bottom with Nahum and Habakkuk like everybody else in the class.

He also had the most beautiful voice you ever heard. "Clear as a bell," Grandmother said. Miss Clarissa thought he was good enough to sing professionally, but he couldn't settle down long enough to do that. Sometimes, he'd sing in the choir at the First Presbyterian Church, but even Miss Annie Grace, the organist who was really nice, got upset if he flapped his arms in his choir robe like they were wings.

As we walked back to my house through the orchard, the sky grew pink and cold. There was a feeling of ice up under the trees. Bubba and I stood in the drive waiting for Obie, who'd stopped at the fence. He seemed to have forgotten that he wanted to come home with me. Suddenly, in a loud voice he called, "'I heard the noise of their wings like the noise of great waters!'" Then he and Icarus were running again, disappearing into the pecan orchard. And Bubba and I were left wondering exactly where he'd gone.

CHAPTER 2

I waved good-bye to Bubba and Lucky and went in the side door. Inside, the house was warm and smelled like peach cobbler.

Nearly everybody in town referred to our house as "the old Holcomb place." It had belonged to my grandfather. Now I lived there with my daddy, Armistead Holcomb, my sister, Claire, and my grandmother. My daddy said that it seemed like nobody ever left the old place or if they did, they always came back, returning like martins to the gourd. He'd left when he first married my mama, and moved to Atlanta to work for the newspaper there. She died when I was just a baby, and he brought me and Claire back home. When Miss Clarissa married Mr. Joyful, they moved to the next house over from us. Even though the pecan orchard was in between us, she could still see the white house with its dark shutters from her windows.

Tom, Grandmother's fat, yellow cat, was sitting in front of the fire. He took a halfhearted swipe at Lucky as we passed. In the hall, the telephone was ringing off the hook. It was Miss Clarissa.

"Where's Obie?" she asked. But before I could even answer, she said, "Never mind. He just walked in." Then she hung up without even saying good-bye.

"What a pain," I said to Lucky.

In the kitchen, Virgie was making Lucky's hoecake. Standing at the stove, she stirred vegetables and bits of meat left over from dinner into a black iron skillet. Then she added cornmeal and gravy and fried it all up together. It was about the last thing she did before leaving for the day.

"That smells good enough for people to eat," I said.

"It's good food," said Virgie, "it's just all mixed up." Virgie Henderson had worked for Grandmother since before I was born, and I loved her. She and her husband, Enoch, lived in the hollow down below our house.

Without even turning around, Virgie said, "Go wash up now. You can set the table for me. And comb that messy hair."

I did as I was told, or as I was ordered. I don't know why Virgie worried about my hair so much. It always looked just the same. I looked at myself in the bathroom mirror. Last summer's freckles still dusted the bridge of my nose so I figured they were there to stay. My hair was brown and straight as a stick. Maybe I needed a home permanent. Ruth Anne Ramsey from school had got one and she said all you had to do was have somebody roll your hair on little rods and then squirt some smelly stuff over your head, and in a little while you got curly hair.

"Where's Grandmother?" I asked, going into the dining room for the silverware.

"Over to Miss Clarissa's," replied Virgie. She covered the bowl of potato salad with waxed paper, then placed it and the platter of fried chicken on the kitchen table. "She's helping your aunt with the new chickens, but she'll be home directly."

Virgie hung her apron on a hook near the pantry door and switched on the back porch light. "I'm leaving now."

She had no sooner walked out the back door when Grandmother came in the side one. Tom followed her in like he always did. She was the only one he loved.

"Hey, darlin'," she said, emptying the pockets of her old tan cardigan of waxed paper twists filled with brown sweet-pea seeds. "I didn't finish getting these planted." In the soft light, the silver in her brown, windblown hair was nearly invisible. She wore white socks and her loafers were muddy. "Where is everybody?"

"Virgie just left, Armistead's not home yet, and I don't know where Claire is. Off flirting somewhere, I reckon." My sister, who was eighteen, was never on time for anything, anywhere. "Guess what we saw today?"

"Cedar waxwings?" asked Grandmother, rinsing her hands at the sink. Then she took a canister out of the pantry and began measuring coffee into the pot.

"No, ma'am. Flying Tigers. The real ones, right out in the cornfield."

"Well, isn't that nice?" said Grandmother. "I heard planes, but didn't have time to go look. I was too busy tryin' to keep those biddies from drowning themselves in the water dish."

We were taking the food into the dining room when the cattle gap rumbled like thunder as my daddy, Armistead Holcomb, hurled his truck across it and roared up the drive.

Some people thought I shouldn't be allowed to call my daddy by his first name. "It's not respectful," Miss Clarissa'd said at least a hundred times. But I loved the sound of it and he didn't mind, anyway. Grandmother said I started calling him Armistead before I could even pronounce it.

"Turn on the radio, Tattnall," said Grandmother, hurrying up the stairs to freshen up before supper. "Your daddy'll want to listen to President Roosevelt's fireside chat."

"Don't tell him about the Flying Tigers," I shouted up the stairs to her. "I want to do it."

"Did you see the waxwings today, Armistead?" Grandmother asked at supper. She paid a lot of attention to birds. She seemed to tell time in terms of wings. Like in early spring when the first bobwhites called. "Time to put away the ax," she'd say. "No need to chop wood for another year." In midspring, she'd watch the cedar waxwings swoop through the orchard, then leave before the whippoorwills called across summer fields. In fall, she'd watch wild geese fly in V-formation across the skies.

Armistead shook his head. "We were so busy that the birds came and went, I expect." He spent most of his time at the newspaper office, writing about the war. If he had wanted to go off to serve his country, he had accepted that he could not. In 1944, the government considered his job "important war work."

"I think Obie saw them," I said, handing him the clean wishbone to pull with me. "And we saw real Flying Tigers! They were almost on top of us! I told Bubba that you knew General Chen . . . oit?"

"Right," he said. "I've known him since he was an instructor at Maxwell Field. He was a captain then. As matter of fact, one of his pilots is from right here in this county."

I couldn't believe that there were any real heroes from here in Pinella.

"Who?"

"Michael McIntosh," he said. "His father owns a farm out on the Dairy Road."

Grandmother came back from the kitchen with dessert. The cobbler was still warm, its thick, buttery crust swimming in sugary peach juice.

"How was Obie this afternoon, when he saw the planes?" she asked.

I took a spoonful of the peaches. I knew what she was asking: "Did Obie behave? Did he act up? When he saw the planes did he run around like a chicken with his head cut off?"

"He was real quiet," I said.

CHAPTER 3

Between the time the cedar waxwings came and went, and the whippoorwills arrived, I bet Obie mentioned the Flying Tigers a million times. He kept going off to the cornfield, hoping to see them again. I think he was kind of lonesome, too. He was really glad when school finally let out and summer vacation started. Now I didn't have to go off and leave him by himself.

Obie did go to school for a while, but he just couldn't fit in. He had a hard time reading and if he got sleepy in class, he'd just take a nap. The teachers got tired of him wandering around the room, rolling the maps up and down. Every other day the principal wound up calling Miss Clarissa.

Finally, she got him a tutor, but Obie didn't seem to learn much. Dr. Moss told her he needed to go off to a special school but Miss Clarissa wouldn't hear of it. "I'm not putting my boy in an institution with a bunch of strangers!" she told him.

The early morning sun shone through the tops of the trees, spattering the leaves with gold. As it moved across the sky, it glittered off my mirror and sparked against Obie's window. The back screened door closed with a thump and barely a minute later, the sound of Virgie's voice lifted in song drifted up the stairs.

"I've got a robe, you've got a robe,
All God's children got a robe;
When I get to Heaven, goin' to put on my
robe,
Goin' to shout all over God's Heaven,
Heaven, Heaven,
Everybody's talkin' 'bout Heaven
Ain't goin' there, Heaven, Heaven,
Goin' to shout all over God's Heaven!"

The chorus about not everybody going to heaven was Virgie's favorite part, and she shouted it loud and clear, leaving no doubt about how she felt.

With Virgie's arrival, the day had officially begun. I started counting—*one . . . two . . . three . . . four . . .*

"Tattnall!" she called from the foot of the stairs. "Get up now, it's gettin' late. Remember, you promised to take Obie to the picture show."

For about a minute, I acted like I hadn't heard her. I mean, this was supposed to be my vacation. But it was hopeless. Tom jumped up onto my chest and nearly scared the breath out of me. I pushed him off and got out of bed. He stalked out of the room with his tail up in the air and as he passed Lucky, took a quick swipe at his nose.

"You ought to bite that cat sometimes," I said to Lucky.

"Tattnall!"

"Comin', Virgie. Right now."

When I got downstairs, Armistead was examining the map that hung on the wall over the sideboard in the dining room. There used to be a chart that showed all the birds on the Eastern seaboard. But when the United States entered the war, the map had replaced it. He was still placing tiny flags to show where the Allied troops were and where the fiercest fighting was taking place.

"Our boys are flying over Berlin right now," he said, "dropping bombs from flying fortresses."

He took his place at the table and Grandmother poured coffee. "This will mean an end to Mr. Hitler. We're going to stop that madman!"

My sister breezed in on a cloud of Evening in Paris perfume. It didn't seem fair that Claire should be so pretty. Her blond hair curled loosely on her shoulders in a pageboy and her eyes were as blue as cornflowers, while mine were a color called "hazel." Her eyelashes held tears the way jewelweeds hold rain.

"What's the matter?" I asked.

"Claire's a bit upset this morning," said Grandmother. "Ted's gotten his orders. He'll be leaving soon."

"Well, good for him!" Armistead said, lifting his glass of orange juice in Claire's direction.

She gave him a funny look. Ted Ashton was her current boyfriend. He played football at the University of Alabama, and worked at his father's drugstore during summers and holidays. Soon as he could, he'd joined the navy, even though he had a special deferment since he was an only son and was studying to be a pharmacist.

"So why is she cryin'?" I asked. "She ought to be proud of him. Ted didn't even have to be drafted."

"Why are you all talking about me as if I weren't here?" Claire asked. "I can hear you. And you, Tattnall, are *such* a child. Ted's going to war.

He's going to be a medic and he'll be in danger. Even *you* ought to be able to understand that."

" 'Even *you* ought to be able to understand that,' " I mimicked. "And I'm *not* a child."

"Now, Claire," said Armistead mildly. "Ted's done what he had to do. We need to support him, to send him off in style. He wouldn't want to see you crying."

Claire stood up and threw her napkin on the table. "No one in this house understands *anything!*" she said, and stalked off upstairs.

"Pass the jelly, please, Tattnall," said Armistead.

"Is Claire really in love with Ted?" I asked.

"Don't talk with your mouth full," said Grandmother.

"She appears to be this week."

Virgie came into the room with a fresh batch of hot biscuits. She looked at Claire's untouched plate. "She gonna finish her breakfast?"

"She's too upset," said Grandmother.

"Hogwash," said Armistead. "That girl's bid a fond farewell to at least a dozen young men this year alone. Half the men in this county have gone off to fight. And as I recall, she cried over most of them."

I took the bacon off of Claire's plate. We only got it once a week since it started being rationed, and I didn't see any point in wasting it.

• • •

Green hummingbirds, tiny as thumbnails, hovered over the morning glories that bloomed like blue silk parasols over Obie's back porch. Armistead tapped the truck horn lightly and Miss Clarissa came to the kitchen door, wiping her hands on her apron.

"Obie'll be right there, Brother," she said. In the heat, her dark hair curled softly around her face. "I'm making ketchup. Tell Mama I'll save you all some. There's none to be had at the store. I reckon they're sending it all overseas to the troops."

Obie came out, kissed his mama, and wandered over to the truck. Icarus was right behind him. Dogs weren't allowed at the picture show, but folks made exceptions for Obie and Icarus. They climbed into the front seat and Obie took his dog onto his lap. "We're going to see the Flying Tigers," he said, tucking his paper sack full of silvertip candy at his feet.

"Obie," called Miss Clarissa, "fix your tie, darlin'."

Obie always wore his daddy's white shirts, starched and ironed. And when he was dressed up, he wore a tie that for some reason never stayed under but one side of his collar. Obediently, he fussed with his tie.

Turning the truck around, Armistead said,

"Good grief, son, you must be hot with that thing on. You can take your tie off if you want to."

But Obie wouldn't. It was like part of him, wearing his daddy's old clothes.

As we started down the drive, Miss Clarissa called out. "Tattnall, you all behave, you hear?"

"I don't know why she doesn't just come right out and say it," I grumbled. "You, Tattnall! You keep Obie out of trouble or it'll be all your fault!"

Armistead just shook his head. "Let's go," he said, tearing down the drive, scattering gravel as we went.

As we rode into town, Obie patted his foot, *pat, pat, pat,* against the floorboard. I guess he was excited about seeing John Wayne in a movie about the Flying Tigers. I put my hand on his knee to stop him, but he ignored me. Finally I said, "Obie, stop!"

He looked at me. "Stop what?"

"Stop patting your foot," I said. "It's driving me crazy!"

He threw his head back against the seat with a jerk. "It's me, it's me, O Lord, standing in the need of prayer, not my brother, not my sister, but it's me, O Lord, standing in the need of prayer."

Armistead was still grinning about that when we pulled up in front of the picture show. "If ya'll will come to the office when the picture's over, I'll give you a ride home," he said, handing me some money. "But don't be late. I've got an appointment this evening and I can't wait for you."

After I paid for our tickets, I still had enough change to buy some popcorn. I was saving for a war bond, but the popcorn smelled so good I couldn't resist. Then, leaving Icarus in the lobby and taking Obie's hand, I led the way. The newsreel was on and the theater was black as pitch. We stood for a minute while our eyes adjusted to the darkness. It wasn't crowded, but there were still a good many people there. We found seats in an empty row about halfway down. Pathé News went off and then there was a preview of a Hopalong Cassidy movie. Finally, the main feature began.

From the moment it started, Obie was caught up in the action, living every thrilling minute with his hero, John Wayne, who was a squadron leader with General Chennault. Watching the Flying Tigers fly their missions over China, you couldn't help but feel proud. And with their scary shark faces, the planes looked just like the P-40s that had flown over the cornfield.

As Obie watched John Wayne trying to control one of his hotheaded pilots, he grew more and more excited. The Tigers got $500 for every downed enemy plane. A Japanese plane fell from the skies and before it hit the ground Obie yelled, "Five hundred dollars!"

When the dogfights began and another plane fell into the sea, Obie began aiming an imaginary machine gun at the screen. "Ack, ack, ack, ack, ack! Got him!" he yelled.

From the row in front of us, a lady turned around and said, "Shush, or I'll call an usher!"

"Darn it, Obie," I whispered, embarrassed. "Hush now!" The Tigers returned to base and Obie grew calmer.

"Have some popcorn," I said, hoping to keep him quiet. But he'd no sooner stuck his hand in the box than John Wayne began his mission to blow up a bridge by dropping nitroglycerine from the plane.

The container of nitro fell through the air and the bridge exploded into bits. "Blow 'em to kingdom come!" Obie yelled, leaping from his seat and tossing popcorn into the air.

"Sit down!" I said, grabbing for his shirt. But before I could stop him, he was running down the aisle toward the stage, holding out his arms and buzzing like an airplane.

In an instant, Mrs. Perkins, who was sitting in the second row, stomped up the aisle, her mouth a thin line. I just knew she was going to call the management.

Obie started for the steps at the side of the stage. It looked like he was going to run across the front of the stage where everybody in the whole picture show would see him. But at the last minute, he stopped, turned around, and raced back down the aisle toward the exit. Then he disappeared behind the heavy velvet curtains.

I ran after him, just as Mrs. Perkins came back down the aisle. In the dark theater she bumped smack into me.

"'Scuse me, Miz Perkins," I said.

"Oh!" she yelped, grabbing on to a seat to keep from falling. "Tattnall Holcomb! Wait till I tell your father!" But I didn't wait for anything. I kept running, pushed the heavy curtains apart and looked for Obie. Just then, I heard a commotion inside. Sticking my head out between the curtains, I looked up toward the balcony, where I saw everybody else was looking too.

Obie was sitting close to the railing, throwing silvertips down onto the heads of the people below. "Boom!" he shouted, lobbing another piece of candy at somebody's head. "Boom!"

The kids in the audience were mostly laughing and trying to catch the candy. But every once in a while you'd hear an "ouch," like somebody might've gotten hurt. Billy Ray Tisdell, who was the daytime usher, was throwing candy back at

Obie, and his aim was pretty good. Meanwhile, the grown-ups didn't think it so funny. Mrs. Perkins took it upon herself to represent them. She marched back up the aisle like Sherman marching through Georgia.

Finally, Mr. Arthur, the projectionist, stepped out of his little room and yelled, "If you kids don't quieten down, I'm gon' stop this movie right here and now! And don't even think you'll get a refund!"

I took the stairs, two at a time. By the time I got to Obie, he'd nearly emptied his sack. "Hey!" I said. "Stop that right now! You're gonna throw 'em all away and there won't be any left for Icarus!" I sat down next to him and patted his arm. "Please, Obie."

Just then, one last silvertip hit him in the head, *splat!* He rubbed his head and looked at me. "Okay." He followed me obediently back to our seats. Popcorn was scattered all over from where he'd thrown it. For him, it was as if nothing had happened.

"I'll go get us some more popcorn," I told him. "But you have to promise to be quiet. Promise?"

"Promise," he said, his eyes riveted on the screen.

CHAPTER 4

Icarus was sitting in the lobby near the door, looking out. Opaline Driggers, who sold tickets and worked the popcorn machine, said, "Don't you worry none about Icarus. He's fine." She looked over her shoulder at the door that said MANAGER on it. "And don't worry about that either, Tattnall. Bobby's gone for the day. Besides, Miz Perkins is always complaining about something."

I admired Opaline, who wore her red hair piled into a Betty Grable upsweep. With a flowery, fluffy handkerchief tucked in her breast pocket and pinned with a sparkly V for Victory pin, she seemed really glamorous. She was nice, too. This wasn't the first time somebody had complained about Obie.

"Thanks, Opaline," I said. "It's just that John Wayne is Obie's hero."

"That boy don't always know what's real and what isn't," she said kindly.

The movie ended and folks started coming out to the lobby. Mrs. Perkins came through the door with fire in her eyes, so I ducked into the rest room and gave her time to leave. By the time I got back to Obie, the feature had ended and Hopalong Cassidy, his white hair shining in the western sun, was on. There was a new crowd waiting to watch John Wayne win the war.

"Obie," I said, sitting down and handing him a box of popcorn, "if you cause any more commotion, I'm gonna leave you right here. You hear me?"

He nodded, intent on the movie.

"Besides, we can't stay for the whole picture again, even if we did miss some of it."

A little while later I said, "C'mon, Obie, let's go now." But he just shook his head and stared straight ahead. So I sat there, waiting for John Wayne to drop that confounded nitroglycerine and praying Obie wouldn't cause another scene.

THE END

BUY WAR BONDS AND STAMPS AT THIS THEATER

flashed on the screen and the lights came on.

The lobby was empty except for Icarus. Opaline had shut down the ticket window and turned off the popcorn machine. The picture show was closed until later that evening.

We went out into the hot glare of late afternoon. Most of the stores along Main Street had closed, the post office blinds were down, and the truck farmers had left the courthouse square. Even the newspaper office was dark. Armistead's truck was gone.

"Aw heck, Obie. It looks like we'll have to walk home."

It was a long way, too, through town, out to the highway, and down the highway for a couple of miles. Then I saw Ted Ashton's black Ford parked in front of the drugstore.

"Hey!" I said. "I bet Ted'll give us a ride. He's probably going out to see Claire, anyway." I figured he'd want to stay on my good side, since he was dating my sister.

Obie sat down on the curb to peel a silvertip for Icarus.

"You're lucky you have some left," I grumbled.

Just then, the three Tuten brothers came around the corner of the courthouse. You only had to look at them to know they were up to no good. They were the town bullies and spent their time making life miserable for kids smaller or younger than they were.

"It's the rootin', pukin' Tutens, Obie. Quick, get up!"

But it was too late. He didn't see the three boys until they were nearly on top of him. Their shadows loomed large against the sidewalk.

"Wellsireebob," said P. J., who at sixteen was the oldest. "If'n it ain't tacky ol' Tattnall and the dummy!" He laughed, proud of his so-called wit. He looked over at Obie. "How 'bout givin' us that candy you're feeding that there dawg?"

All three boys were shirtless, their overalls filthy and their bare feet crusted with dirt. "Dummy, dummy, dummy!" chanted Junior and Cluster in unison. Obie stood up, confused by their loudness. They drew closer to him, making smaller and smaller circles around him and snatching at the paper sack of candy. Obie turned first one way, then another, watching them.

"You shut up and leave him alone!" I said. "He's not hurting you."

" 'You shut up,' " the boys mimicked in high voices. " 'You bad ol' boys!' " They hooted and jeered, punching one another and laughing. They smelled rank and hot. As they moved closer, Icarus growled and bared his teeth. The boys backed away.

"If'n that dawg bites me, my pa'll sue you," threatened P. J.

"Then you just better leave Obie alone, or I'll sic Icarus on you," I said. "He's a trained killer."

P. J. stood still for a minute, watching Icarus warily. Obie stood up, the crumpled paper sack in one hand. His tie was crooked, his right foot held at an angle. Suddenly, Junior pushed him, catching him off balance. Icarus growled, a menacing sound low in his throat.

"My pa said Obie's a dummy, and that's what he is," said P. J.

"Yeah," said Junior. "He cain't even walk straight."

"I betcha he's a monster," said Cluster, pushing my shoulder hard enough to hurt. "How come you want to run around with a monster?" He began walking like Frankenstein's monster, stiff-legged, his arms held out in front of him. His brothers laughed at him, their voices loud and jeering.

Obie wore a lost look that just about broke my heart. My arms began to prickle like there were pins sticking in them and the pavement felt hot under my feet. I had trouble catching my breath. Without even thinking, I ran straight at Cluster and butted him squarely in the stomach. He sprawled back against the pavement.

"Now it's your turn, Junior," I shouted. "I'm gonna knock the pee-winding stew out of you!"

Junior held both hands in front of his face, trying to duck. Then Cluster got up off the sidewalk, furious that I'd knocked him down. "Come on," he screamed. "Let's get her!"

I kicked his shins as hard as I could with the heel of my sandal, and he doubled up in pain. Icarus rushed for Junior's ankles and Obie was swinging his arms in all directions, flailing about like a windmill. He lost his balance and fell to one knee. P. J. grabbed my arm and I bit down hard on his dirty hand.

Suddenly, the side of my head exploded and the sidewalk rushed up to meet me. P. J. had knocked the wind right out of me. The whole world turned red. Bile rose up in my throat, hot and stinging. Icarus was barking and barking but it seemed to come from a long way off.

When I looked up, P. J. was sailing backward through the air. *I didn't know he could fly,* I thought blearily. And Ted Ashton stood on the sidewalk, his face white with rage. "That's enough!" he barked. "You boys get up and get out of here. And if I ever catch you bothering Obie or Tattnall again, I'll break your scrawny little necks!"

I'd never been so glad to see anybody in my

whole life. Ted looked bigger, better, and handsomer than anyone I'd ever laid eyes on. He looked like a hero.

All three boys ran toward the courthouse. At the corner, P. J. slowed slightly and turned around. "My pa'll sue you!" he yelled. "He ain't scairt of nothin'!"

"Oh yeah?" I hollered. "Well, if he's so brave, how come he ain't in the army?"

CHAPTER 5

The drugstore smelled like vanilla ice cream. Slow-turning ceiling fans were reflected in the gleaming marble of the counters. There was a sign over the soda fountain listing various drinks and sodas:

BLACKOUT SUNDAE (DARK AS PITCH)
PARATROOP SUNDAE (GOES DOWN EASY)
VICTORY SPLASH! (HOORAY FOR OUR SIDE)

Ted switched on the lights. "Wait here for a minute while I call your folks," he said. "Then after I get Tattnall cleaned up, I'll fix you all whatever you want to eat."

Obie sat at the fountain, turning round and round on a stool. I looked at myself in the mirror. My dress was torn, my eye looked all puffy, and my right ear was bright red. I could taste blood inside my bottom lip. I tried to smooth my hair but it was hopeless. I was a mess.

"What did they say?" I asked when Ted came back.

"I explained what happened," Ted said. "Mrs. Holcomb was worried, but she's okay. Miss Clarissa didn't take it too well, though."

I'd already figured on that.

"Hold this against your ear," said Ted, handing me a pad soaked with witch hazel.

"How come those boys are always so mean to Obie?" I asked as Ted swabbed my knees with salve.

"Because they're just ignorant children," he said. "They don't know any better because they weren't taught any better. It's easy to hate somebody who's different."

"Well, I hate *them,*" I said.

"Hate what they do," said Ted. "They're not worth hating."

He checked Obie over, but nothing seemed to be hurt except his pride.

I went over to the cosmetics counter. It always seemed like such a mysterious place, full of bottles and jars and creams. "Can I try some of this stuff?" I asked, picking up a tester of perfume.

"Have a ball," said Ted, touching Obie's cut cheek lightly with Mercurochrome.

But when I sprayed the perfume on my neck, it stung from the scratches. I had a hard time finding a spot that didn't hurt, so I sprayed my dress, mostly. I wanted to try out some of the creams and lotions, exotic in their pale containers, but I didn't know if I should open them.

After Ted put everything back in place, we went over to the soda fountain. As we sat down, Obie looked over at me and held his nose.

"Phew!" he said.

"Phew yourself," I said. "What's wrong?"

"You smell like Catawba worms."

"Sometimes you're such a drip, Obie," I said. "Girls are *supposed* to smell good."

"What *is* that smell, Tattnall?" Ted asked, a funny look on his face.

"Just a little bit of everything," I said, giving him my best smile.

"Good grief," he said softly.

I wondered what I'd done wrong. Maybe you weren't supposed to wear but one kind at a time. Then I figured that maybe Ted just didn't like perfume.

"Okay," Ted said, grinning. "You two name your poison."

We both chose Blackout Sundaes—chocolate ice cream and chocolate syrup topped with pecans and chocolate sprinkles. Ted gave Icarus a dip of vanilla ice cream in a bowl. Even though it was delicious, I couldn't finish mine, but Obie ate every last bite of his, then tipped the bowl up and drank all the sweet liquid. When he finished, he looked at me in the mirror over the fountain. He reached out a finger and lightly touched the bruise over my eye.

"Ouch," I said. "Don't!"

"That hurt?" he asked, looking like I'd hurt *him*.

"Yeah, it does," I said, more gently.

He closed his eyes, and the lids seemed almost transparent. "Sorry," he said.

Ted drove us home through the warm summer evening. The sweet scent of grass and honeysuckle drifted in through the car windows. Obie began to sing:

"Mine eyes have seen the glory of
the coming of the Lord;
He is tramping out the vintage where
the grapes of wrath are stored;
He has loosed the fateful lightning of

His terrible swift sword;
His truth is marching on."

It was the song the movie had ended with. At the chorus, Ted joined in, his voice soft and low but strong:

"Glory, glory, hallelujah!
Glory, glory, hallelujah!
Glory, glory, hallelujah!
His truth is marching on!"

When we got to Obie's house, Miss Clarissa was waiting on the porch. I could tell she was mad even before she said anything. And I was willing to bet that she'd already been on the phone to Grandmother complaining about my behavior.

Ted walked up the steps with Obie, and Miss Clarissa took her son into the light where she could see better. She patted his face, said something to Ted, then started down the steps.

I got out of the backseat. I didn't want her fussing at me in the car. There were butterflies in my stomach and all that sweet syrup was beginning to make me queasy.

"I just don't understand you, young lady," she said before I could even close the door. "Fighting on a public street! And look at you!"

"But, Miss Clarissa, it wasn't my fault," I said. "Those boys—"

She wasn't about to let me finish. "One of my friends happened to be riding by and saw you, missy. And don't think I haven't already spoken with your grandmother! Oh, yes. She knows all about it. You know, Tattnall, it's beginning to look like every time you and Obie go someplace, you get him into trouble. Now, I've tried to make allowances . . . with your poor mama gone . . . but I'm beginning to think you can't be trusted."

I opened my mouth to say something, but nothing would come out.

Suddenly, from where he stood on the porch, Obie roared, "'For He shall give his angels charge over thee. To keep thee in all thy ways.'"

For a moment, no one moved or spoke. Then Obie reached down, picked up his dog, and went into the house.

We all watched as the door closed behind him. In a moment, Ted said softly, "What I think Obie's trying to say, Miss Clarissa, is that Tattnall was trying to protect him." Then he and I got into his car and he drove slowly down the drive.

"It's not fair!" I told him, trying not to cry. "I'm always taking care of Obie, watching out for him. But she doesn't even see that. She always blames me when something bad happens to him." I bit down on my bottom lip to keep from crying, but it hurt and the tears rushed to my eyes.

"You aren't responsible for Obie," said Ted, handing me a clean white handkerchief. "Don't be so hard on yourself."

He parked in the drive and as we walked into the house he asked, "How often does Obie quote Scripture like that?"

"He's been doing it more and more," I said. "What he just said about angels? That's from the Ninety-first Psalm we were reading in Sunday school. I guess he remembers it."

Inside, Grandmother examined my eye and ear and thanked Ted for being so kind to Obie and me. Claire was nice too, but I knew she was just trying to impress Ted.

"We saved your supper," said Grandmother.

But I was too full of Blackout Sundae and besides, my stomach felt peculiar, like I might throw up. When I excused myself to go upstairs, Ted said good night and kissed my cheek, and I thought, *I'm going to love him for the rest of my life.*

Fireflies starred the garden. And from my window, I could see the light in Obie's room. I thought about what he'd said there on the porch, about angels keeping him. I knew he meant me.

He thought that I'd protected him, and that I always would. The idea made me uncomfortable, and I turned away from the window.

Lucky came over, put his head on the window seat, and looked up at me. That's when I started to cry. Too many things had happened, with Obie's scene at the picture show and the fight, and Miss Clarissa screaming at me. I thought about Obie with that candy. He'd thrown it too hard, like he wasn't kidding. That part bothered me the most.

I wiped my eyes on the hem of my gown and Lucky moved his head onto my knee, his muzzle as soft as velvet. His eyes were brown and liquid-looking and that made me cry even harder. "Oh, Lucky," I said, laying my head on top of his. "I'm worried about Obie."

CHAPTER 6

The thick vines of the scuppernong arbor made a house of green shade. Bumblebees droned sleepily in and out of the leaves. I was reading *Little Women* for the third time. Beth was dying and Jo's heart was breaking. I wiped my eyes on the tail of my shirt, being careful not to wipe too hard.

"Tattnall? Where are you, Tattnall?"

Zinnia's whiny little voice floated on the air. Peering through the leaves, I could see Bubba's sister coming down the back path. Zinnia was ten, not quite two years younger than me, but she acted like a baby. I tried to scrunch down so she wouldn't see me, but it was no use.

A moment later, she spotted me.

"Hey," she said, brushing past the trailing vines. Her freckled face was smeared with chocolate and crumbs. Her glasses gave her a wise, owl-like look. "Whatcha doin'?"

"Oh, hey, Zinnia," I mumbled, closing my book.

"Your eyes are all squinchy," she said. "How come?"

"I was reading," I told her. "And my eye's still swollen from the fight." Zinnia would never understand crying over Beth.

She squatted down and peered closely at me. In the deep shade her skin looked pale green. "You shouldn't fight," she said, squinting. She looked around the arbor, then down at my book. "You gonna read that whole thing?"

I didn't give her the satisfaction of an answer.

Scratching absently at the mosquito bites that peppered her legs, Zinnia said, "I don't know why you want to read all the time. Let's go play something."

I gave up. "You could at least say you're sorry about my eye," I said.

"Oh. I'm sorry. Aw, here comes Obie," said Zinnia as we walked down the path to my house. "He don't even know how to play games. What's he want?"

I hadn't seen Obie since the day of the fight. Miss Clarissa had been keeping him close to home. "You be nice to him or we won't play anything," I told her.

Obie walked jerkily toward us, his sweet face pale in the dappled shade of the trees.

"He looks funny," said Zinnia.

"Does not," I said, waiting for him.

"Does too," said Zinnia.

"Does not."

"Does too."

"Well, shut up about it," I said as Obie drew near. "You'll hurt his feelings."

Obie walked over to me and held out his hand. A streak of blue, as tender as the summer sky, lay on his palm.

"Aw, that's nothin' but a feather," said Zinnia.

Obie looked at me, then touched the feather lightly to my eye.

" 'He shall cover thee with his feathers,' " he quoted.

"Huh?" said Zinnia. Then looking at my eye more closely, she announced, "That thing looks like it's in Technicolor. It's all green and yellow and squirmy brown." She'd given it short shrift before, but if Obie was interested, then she was too. "Yessir," she declared. "That is a sickenin'-lookin' eye, all right."

I tucked the bluebird's feather into my shirt pocket. "Thanks, Obie," I said. "Now let's go. Maybe Virgie'll give us some lemonade and cookies."

"She already gave me some," said Zinnia smugly.

We sat out on the screened porch, playing Fish. Both dogs were lying on their stomachs, hassling in the heat. The backs of my legs were sticking to the slick cushions of the glider, and by the time we finished arguing over the final game, my ears hurt from Zinnia's whining. I was glad to see her go home.

The overhead fan turned slowly, stirring the warm air, which smelled of grass. In the garden, blue jays splashed in the birdbath, chasing the sparrows away. A truck passed on the road.

"Tattnall," said Obie, watching the birds. "Did you ever wish you could fly?"

"Sure," I said. Then I thought a moment. "Do you mean like wishing you could *really* fly or like a pilot?"

He shrugged. "I don't know. If I had wings I could fly."

"Where would you go?" I asked.

"To the sky," he said, looking at me as if I'd asked a silly question.

He reached into his paper sack and took out two silvertips. Peeling off the foil, he handed me the wrappers and gave the candy to Icarus and Lucky. The Junior Services Corps at school was collecting tinfoil as part of the war effort.

"I wish I could fly," he said again.

And in that instant, I wished that he could too. I wished that he could soar far above the people who were mean to him or made fun of him to a place where he was free.

CHAPTER 7

"What's a doughnut girl?" I asked when Claire said at breakfast that she was going to be one.

"We work in the canteen," she said with a toss of her hair. "We keep up morale."

"Can I be one?" I asked.

"Darlin'," she said, smiling beatifically at me, "with that black eye and cauliflower ear, you'd have those boys thinkin' we were losin' the war."

"Ha, ha," I said, eyeing the platter of eggs and bacon. There was one strip left and I wanted it, but I wasn't fast enough. Quick as lightning, Claire speared it, her fork held daintily in slender pink-tipped fingers. She talked slow but she was fast.

"Tattnall's doing her part for the home front," said Armistead mildly, "which, I might say, is more than you're doing."

"What?" Claire asked, taking a teensy bite of toast. "Whatever do you mean?"

"Jimmy Ray Leeds is what," he said, taking a helping of scrambled eggs.

"He's coming all the way from Memphis with his band," Claire protested. "And all I'm doin' is introducing him at the canteen. It's not like a *date*."

"Does Ted know?" I asked, pleased to give her a hard time while Armistead was on my side.

"I have to do my part for the war effort, don't I?" she asked, batting her long eyelashes and ignoring me. Her eyes were as blue as the cotton pinafore she wore over her crisp white blouse.

I knew it. She couldn't be true to anybody. She just wanted to get dressed up so everybody could see her. It made me mad that she couldn't see how wonderful Ted was. She didn't deserve him, in my opinion.

"I don't have any objections to your doing something for the war effort," said Armistead, "but being on a stage with Jimmy Ray Leeds is not my idea of helping. And why is it he's not in the service? I believe that boy's a draft dodger, just like most of those fellas in show business."

"Why, he is not either," said Claire with a pout. "He tried to join the army, but they wouldn't take him 'cause he's got flat feet."

"Wouldn't *have* him is more like it," muttered Armistead. "Besides, it's not his feet I object to, it's his brain. Or the lack of it. And I fail to understand how you can be crying over Ted one minute, then going out with a draft-dodger the next."

He reached for the butter dish. Looking hard at the yellow and white mixture in the dish, he asked, "What the Sam Hill is this stuff?"

"Now, Armistead," said Grandmother, coming in from the kitchen with fresh coffee. "Don't get excited. That's margarine. I couldn't get any butter this week. There *is* a war on, you know."

"I *know* there's a war on! That's what this is all about! Claire wants to date that sorry piece of work and this goop has streaks in it. The confounded *cows* haven't gone to war, have they?"

"Armistead," said Grandmother, a bit tartly. "It takes all my red-point ration stamps for one week to buy even a half pound of butter. And since yellow margarine costs ten cents more a pound than white, we buy the white and mix it ourselves."

"Well, it's not mixed right!" he said. "We'll do without, thank you. Virgie," he called, "would you be so kind as to remove this abomination from the table. It's not fit for human consumption."

Virgie came in, removed the butter dish, and went back into the kitchen, shaking her head.

A moment later, Claire said sweetly, "I don't think you're being very nice this morning, Papa. It's our patriotic duty to support the war effort."

Boy, I thought. *Sometimes Claire is really dumb*. And when did she start that "Papa" stuff? It was always "Daddy" up till now. Even I knew that he wasn't mad about the margarine. He was upset with her because of Ted.

Calmly, he folded his napkin. "Claire," he said. "If you want to go to a dance with Flatfoot Jimmy with the floy-floy, you go right ahead. Although, it seems to me you ought to be more concerned about Ted's leaving than that crooner's arriving. Jimmy Ray is so dense that if brains were broadcloth, he wouldn't have enough to make a pissant a veil." With that he got up from the table and left the room. The side door slammed and a minute later the pickup truck started with a roar.

Virgie eased the kitchen door open. She was biting her bottom lip the way she always did when she was trying not to laugh. As soon as I saw her, I knew it was hopeless. She started to giggle, then Grandmother began to laugh, her head thrown back, her eyes closed. Claire flushed deeply and stormed up the stairs.

The next afternoon, I was sitting on the end of Claire's bed, watching as she got ready for her date. She'd changed her mind about going to the canteen to introduce Jimmy and was going to a picture show in Selma with Ted. The radio was on and a lady was singing, "I'll Get By." Claire was humming softly as she sat at her dresser, putting on her makeup. A warm breeze swelled the white ruffled curtains, revealing the treetops.

"How come you're home early from the bank? I asked, watching as she delicately spit in the mascara box, then applied the black stuff to her eyelashes.

"It's Wednesday," said Claire. "The bank's closed half-day. I declare, you need to pay attention to what's goin' on in the world, Tattnall."

Claire had worked at the bank ever since she left the university after only one year. She wasn't interested in working at the newspaper. She planned to get married, and that's all she'd ever planned to do. I figured the real reason she left school was because she didn't get to be Homecoming Queen the first year, but I can't prove it.

"Can I try that?" I asked. Claire looked a little surprised, but she made room for me on the bench.

"Come on," she said. "I guess it's time you learned how." She watched as I brushed the eyelashes of my good eye with the little brush. It wasn't as easy as it looked and I got more under my eye than on it. Handing me a tissue, she said, "Take it off before Grandmother sees you. She'll have a hissy fit. You don't need *two* black eyes—you look like a raccoon."

"If I was grown," I said, "I wouldn't work in a tacky ol' bank. I'd work in an airplane factory."

Claire looked at me in the mirror. Then she picked up an eyelash curler and pressed it to her thick eyelashes. "Honestly, Tattnall," she said with one eye closed. "To begin with, there isn't an airplane factory within a hundred miles of Pinella, and even if there were, I couldn't get enough gas to go if I wanted to. Hand me that leg makeup from the bureau, would you? Ted will be here any minute."

"So what?" I said, passing her the small, round case that held the makeup. "He's used to waiting for you. What changed your mind about going to the canteen with Flatfoot Jimmy?"

She handed me the eyelash curler. "Try this," she said. "Just the good eye."

When I finished, she looked at me. "Not bad." Turning from her dressing table, she said, "Ted's a wonderful man. *That's* what changed my mind."

She began smoothing the makeup over her legs. Then she went over to the full-length mirror on the door. "I wish I could draw a seam down the back," she said, looking over her shoulder at her legs.

"I can do it!" I said.

"You sure?"

"Better than you can backward," I replied.

When I was done, she sprayed herself with perfume.

"I happen to know Ted doesn't like perfume," I said authoritatively, remembering what he'd said to me in the drugstore. But Claire just stuck her tongue out at me and tippytoed down the stairs.

I heard her yelp as she reached the landing. Tom waited there, hidden from any unsuspecting victim. He'd pounce, grab your ankles, and scare you silly. Armistead said he had so many holes in his trousers from Tom's claws that he had his own ventilation system.

"Aren't you glad you weren't wearing real stockings?" I yelled.

"Shut up!" said Claire, slamming the front door behind her.

• • •

Two days later, Claire announced her engagement to Ted. And then, it was like everybody in the family went flat crazy. There had to be an engagement party before Ted left for the navy, so, as Armistead said, "All the troops were called in."

Miss Clarissa promised to make her Lady Baltimore cake, which was famous throughout the county. Virgie searched cookbooks for new recipes, and for the ration stamps to make them possible. Grandmother was busily sewing the "perfect" dress for Claire. I hoped that Claire realized how lucky she was to be engaged to Ted.

"Gonna be fair!" was the pronounced judgment of everybody who stepped outside the house to look up at the sky, and I began to think that engagement parties, like ball games, could be called on account of rain.

As I walked across the living room the day of the party, the heels of my black patent-leather shoes clicked against the polished floor. The rugs had been rolled back and the floor freshly waxed for dancing. In the cool, empty room, I twirled around so that the skirt of my pink organdy dress puffed out like a flower. I closed my eyes and pretended that the party was for me, and that I'd be the most popular girl there. Then the doorbell rang as the first guests arrived, and I escaped into the dining room to check out the food before it got picked over.

A recording of the Mills Brothers singing "Till Then" drifted out to the kitchen, where Virgie was overseeing everything from her command post. Obie and I were keeping her company after Grandmother had said "Don't get underfoot" when she saw us in the dining room. I didn't think I *was* underfoot. It wasn't my fault Obie followed me every step. Maybe if I could have hung around, somebody would have asked me to dance. Although that was doubtful. My new Mary Janes made my feet look like gunboats, and my dress was already wrinkled at the back.

Ted came into the kitchen. He looked different. His blond hair was real short and you could see his scalp through it.

"Is there a young lady in here who would honor me with a dance?" he said.

For a minute, nobody said anything. Then Virgie looked over at me and grinned. "He means you, sweetheart," she said. I stood up from the table, nearly knocking my glass of lemonade over.

We danced the four-step while I counted in my head. I only stepped on Ted's feet twice, and both times he apologized. He smelled like Old Spice shaving lotion. Claire watched us, smiling, looking beautiful in her sky blue dress.

When we were done, Ted asked Obie to come with us out to his car in the drive. Stars were scattered thick as sequins in the night sky, and magnolia blossoms scented the air. Reaching into the backseat of his black Ford coupe, he took out his Alabama football sweater.

"I'd like you to keep this for me," he said, draping it over Obie's thin shoulders. In the light that spilled from the porch, the sweater was the color of American Beauty roses.

Obie rubbed his hands down over the sleeves. "It shall be my shield and buckler," he said.

Ted smiled. "That's from the Psalms, isn't it?" he asked.

"I don't remember," said Obie.

Upstairs, Obie admired himself in the long mirror in Grandmother's room. "How do I look?" he asked.

He stood very still. His cowlick was sticking straight up on the back of his head. The sweater was big enough to wrap around him twice.

"Fine, Obie," I said. "You look just fine."

Then, turning to me, he saluted before he marched off to the kitchen to show Virgie.

CHAPTER 8

The next day, Ted left for the navy, and the summer of 1944 kicked into full swing. Armistead worked longer and longer hours at the paper, and Claire, for the first time in her life, took up the pen. She began writing letters to Ted on thin, pale blue airmail stationery. She put a drop of perfume on each envelope.

"She's gonna stink up the whole United States Post Office," I said, handing the letters to Armistead to mail in town. He just raised his eyebrows, put the letters in the breast pocket of his seersucker suit, and left for the newspaper office. As I watched him tear off down the drive, I kind of wished I had somebody to write to. There were probably lots of soldiers and sailors who'd love to hear from a girl back home like me.

One afternoon, Armistead didn't come home. In late evening, Grandmother took his supper down to the office. The next morning, he brought us a copy of the paper. It was dated June 6, and the headline read:

D DAY: THE GREAT INVASION IS UNDER WAY

"Our Allied troops have landed in Normandy, in France," said Armistead, red-eyed from working all night. As he talked about what the invasion meant, he said wistfully, "Just imagine all those ships in formation on the seas. It must have been a glorious thing to see. There were seven hundred ships and four thousand landing craft. It was the largest armada ever."

At church on Sunday, the Reverend Allen said that everyone needed to pray for peace; a terrible naval battle was being fought and men were dying. The congregation stood to sing "The Mariners' Hymn," and when the last lines rang out, "O hear us when we cry to Thee, For those in peril on the sea," Claire wept silently. The next day, she gave notice at the bank and went to work at the newspaper office. "I have to do something that means something," she said.

Armistead was delighted. "I knew all along that you weren't just another pretty face," he said, and put her straight to work.

One morning early, I was on the back porch getting buckets for Obie and me. Grandmother was making blackberry jelly and had offered to buy all the berries we could pick. I always needed money. Obie never earned any, 'cause he ate every berry he found, but he still liked to go.

"Don't ya'll be goin' down there less'n you take a big stick," Virgie warned from the kitchen door. "You got to watch out for snakes. They're movin' in July. And Tattnall, go put on a long-sleeve shirt and some socks. Those chiggers will eat you up."

Obie arrived wearing a long-sleeve shirt buttoned up to the neck and Ted's red sweater. When I came downstairs after changing, Virgie had peanut-butter sandwiches and peach tarts in a bag for us.

"There's a Mason jar full of cold lemonade in the icebox out back," she told me. "And Obie, leave your sweater here. It's too hot to be wearin' it." She stood at the back door with her hand out.

He seemed to be thinking it over, then he shook his head. "It's my sword and buckler," he said.

"Lord, chile," said Virgie, going back into the kitchen.

We headed down a path that led past Virgie's house. Her husband Enoch's garden lay green and lush in the sun. Every row was perfect. "Enoch plants the way the Indians did," I told Obie. But he wasn't interested.

There was no sign of Enoch, but his tools were lined up neatly along the side of the barn, like they were waiting for him. We walked down to where Hard Labor Creek went underground and the best blackberry vines grew. Obie held an empty bucket in each hand, and with every step he took, he'd hit each knee with it. He sounded like a parade.

"Obie," I said. "Why don't you put the little bucket inside the big bucket and carry 'em that way?"

"I don't have to if I don't want to," he said, smiling.

"Fine, fine, fine," I said, even though the noise was getting on my nerves.

When we reached the first patch of blackberry bushes, I said, "You start here. I'll go up a little ways." I put the picnic basket in the shade of a tree and went farther into the woods.

My bucket was nearly full by the time the sun was directly overhead. I was getting hungry and my waist was starting to itch, which meant I probably had chiggers. I walked back and found Obie about where I'd left him. Only instead of picking berries, he was asleep, his back against the trunk of a big pine tree. Icarus lay next to him. I went to get the picnic basket, thinking about how useless Obie was sometimes. He could at least have picked up our lunch before he took a nap.

I found a level spot and laid out the cloth. Then, as I was smoothing the edges, my hand nearly touched something. A snake was sticking out from under Icarus!

For a moment, I couldn't move. It was like my hand was frozen. The snake was dark gray but I couldn't see its markings with Icarus right on top of most of it. I only saw the narrow head and the eyes, which were like shiny bits of coal. I took a deep breath and slowly, slowly stood up.

Obie was still asleep. I wanted to scream at him, to shake him till his teeth rattled, but I was afraid to move. The snake was real still. *Maybe it's dead,* I thought. Then . . . *zip!* . . . the little forked tongue cut through the air. My breath caught in my throat.

Icarus opened one eye sleepily, scratched behind an ear, and made himself more comfortable. My heart was thudding so hard I was afraid

I'd have a heart attack, and the woods were so quiet that the silence rang in my ears. I moved ever so slowly backward, trying not to make a sound. I didn't know what to do! Too late I remembered Virgie's warning about taking a big stick. I looked around to find something to hit the snake with, but there was nothing except fallen pine branches so brittle they'd break in your hand. Then I thought about Enoch's hoe leaning against the side of the barn.

I turned and raced back to the path. *Please don't let anybody move till I get back, please, please, please . . .*

With the hoe in my hand, I tiptoed up to where Obie and Icarus were sleeping.

"Obie," I said softly, trying to make him hear me without screaming, "Obie, wake up."

He opened his eyes. "You got a hoe," he said.

"Obie, you got to get up real easy. Easy as you can."

"Okay," he said, standing up.

"Now, move over here to me. Easy! You see that?" I said, pointing to the dark-striped snake.

"What you gonna do with that hoe?" he asked. Just then, Icarus opened one eye, looked at Obie, and went back to sleep.

Sweat trickled down the small of my back and a cloud of gnats flew into my eyes and ears.

"If that dumb dog'll move, I'm gonna get that snake he's laying on," I said.

"Oh," said Obie. He went over to Icarus and began pulling at his collar.

"No!" I said. "Don't—" But before I could stop him, Obie started dragging Icarus off the snake.

"Okay," he said. "Now you can get it." And he stood off to one side, the snake only inches from his feet. The next thing I knew, Obie actually kneeled down to get a closer look. When he looked back up at me, his eyes were shiny, glittery. A thin line of sweat glistened on his upper lip.

"Get away from there. Now!" I ordered. "Don't you know what you're doing?"

"You want to pet him?" Obie asked, reaching for the snake.

It slithered closer to his feet.

Lord help me, I prayed. I lifted the hoe, closed my eyes, and brought it down with all my strength. When I opened my eyes, the snake was nowhere to be seen.

"Where'd it go?"

"Gone," said Obie. "You missed. But it was a pretty fast snake."

I looked around to be sure it wasn't just waiting to strike me dead, but I didn't see it anywhere.

My legs were trembling so hard that I had to sit down. I rested my head on my knees.

"Obie," I said, when I could speak. "Don't you realize you and Icarus could've been snake-bit?"

He looked at me and smiled. "Not while I'm wearin' my sweater," he said sweetly.

All the way back home I was so mad I couldn't even talk to Obie. *What if I hadn't been there?* I kept thinking. What then? Was it my job to always watch out for him and make sure he didn't get hurt? Well, if it was, it was too much, and I was sick and tired of it.

He ran ahead of me, his arms held straight out as he dipped and swooped through the Queen Anne's lace that grew waist-high. "Obie!" I yelled. "Sometimes you really make me mad!"

In the kitchen, I put the blackberries in the sink and went upstairs to check for chiggers. When I came back down, I found Virgie in the backyard hanging out the wash.

"There you are," she said. "I saw your blackberries, and that hoe you left near the steps where I could fall and break my neck."

"It's Enoch's," I said. "I kinda borrowed it."

"Well, I 'spect you'd best kinda take it back," she said, snapping a pillowcase by its corners. "What'd you need a hoe for, anyway?"

I started telling her about the snake. "Obie bent down to *pet* it, if you can believe that," I said. "I whacked at it just in time, and it scooted away."

Virgie looked at me like she could see inside my head, inside my heart. Her big brown eyes were meltingly soft and kind.

"Let's go on inside, sugah. I believe it's time somebody took care of *you* for a change."

In the kitchen, the floor fan turned slowly, stirring the warm air. I sat at the table watching as Virgie made biscuits. The handle of the sifter made a squeaky-squawky sound as the pale flour drifted through, forming a soft mound in the blue mixing bowl. The smell of buttermilk was strong and bitter.

The back door opened and Obie walked in. He was still wearing Ted's red sweater. Sweat glistened at his temples.

"Obie," said Virgie. "Be a good boy and hand those glasses down from the cabinet over the sink. I can't hardly reach that top shelf. And you, Tattnall, go chip us some ice. We need some tea to cool us off."

The old icebox stood on the back porch. After putting a chunk of ice in the enameled dishpan on the drainboard, I chopped it with the ice pick and filled three glasses.

Using the corner of her apron, Virgie took

out a small pan of biscuits from the oven. "Ya'll can have one, but that's all. Dinner's in a little while."

Obie poked a hole in his biscuit and filled it with syrup. Watching him, Virgie said, "Obie, Tattnall tells me ya'll saw a snake this mornin'."

He didn't answer her; he just started rocking in his chair, back and forth, back and forth.

"Obie," I said, "I just want you to tell me, in front of Virgie, how come you weren't scared? Snakes can bite you, you know."

He stopped rocking. "Not while I'm wearin' my sweater," he said.

"It's not Superman's cape," I said.

Virgie got up and went over to him. "You got to be careful, sweet boy, or you can get yourself hurt."

"Not while I'm wearin' my *sweater,"* he repeated, more loudly.

Virgie turned to the window and looked out into the garden. She shook her head, then said, "They do say the Lord tempers the wind to the shorn lamb."

"What's that mean?" I asked.

"It means He takes care of those who can't take care of themselves." She sat back down at the table. Then, patting Obie's hand, she said, "But you got some special gifts, don't you?"

"Yessum," he said. "I got my sweater. That was a special gift from Ted."

"But you got a *really* special gift, Obie," said Virgie. "The Lord gave you a beautiful singing voice."

He licked the syrup off his fingers. "You want me to sing for you?" he asked. "I will."

And sitting at the kitchen table, he began:

"Amazing grace, how sweet the sound
That saved a wretch like me,
I once was lost, but now am found,
Was blind, but now I see."

From outside the kitchen window, the song of a mockingbird rose and fell with liquid grace, mingling with the song Obie sang and rising into the summer air as sweetly as the scent of home-made bread. Virgie listened with her eyes closed.

When Obie finished, she wiped the tears from her eyes with her apron.

"Jesus loves that chile," she said, "to have given him a voice like that."

CHAPTER 9

"There's a Betty Grable movie at the picture show," I said. "Ya'll want to go after supper?" I was mostly talking to Bubba, since I still felt a little mad at Obie.

"That's a girl's picture," said Bubba. "All that singin' and smoochin'. The only movie star I want to see is Roy."

Roy Rogers was Bubba's favorite cowboy, but I only went to cowboy pictures 'cause Bubba liked them. We were sitting outside his daddy's filling station. Bubba and I were playing checkers and Obie was kind of wandering around, looking at things. It was the first time he'd been allowed to go anywhere without his mama since the snake incident. When Miss Clarissa heard about that, she'd about had a hissy fit and kept him close to home. Finally I guess she couldn't stand it anymore so she let him out. But he was jumpy as a cat from being in the house too long.

I went inside to get us some cold drinks. The icy water in the big red icebox numbed my arm as I felt around for Cokes and Obie's strawberry drink. After drying my arm, I got three cellophane packets of peanuts from the stand near the cash register.

"The money's on the counter, Mr. Tarpley," I called. He was lying on his back on a creeper under a car. He wriggled a foot in my direction as I went back outside.

We poured the peanuts into our cold drinks, then shook the bottles, enjoying the mixture of salt and sweetness. Bubba drank fast, swallowing peanuts and Coca-Cola at the same time. Then he stood up and took a deep breath. Freckles dotted his nose. His T-shirt was tight against his plump middle, showing a strip of pale skin.

"Ready?" I asked.

Bubba nodded. He filled his chest with air and then, opening his mouth wide, began to sing and burp at the same time. The burp was long and measured and rumbled through the song.

"Home, home on the raaange,
Where the deer and the antelope plaaay,"

resounded like an erupting volcano. From under the car, Mr. Tarpley said, "Son! You'll scare off the customers!"

"That was a good one," I said, tapping the bottom of my packet to dislodge the last few peanuts. "Bubba," I asked, "do you think I've got pretty legs?"

"Why?" he asked.

"'Cause it would be nice to have pretty legs like Betty Grable."

"I don't think they look as good as Betty Grable's," he said.

"Aw, what do you know?" I said.

"I think they're pretty," Obie put in.

"I'm glad *someone* has taste," I said.

Just then, a sleek white car pulled up in front of the gas pumps. The driver blew the horn and got out. He was dressed all in white, even his shoes. Mr. Tarpley came outside, wiping his hands on a greasy rag.

"How 'bout checking it out for me," the man said. "See what you think. It just don't sound right."

Mr. Tarpley climbed into the front seat and started the engine. When he put his foot on the accelerator, the car backfired with a sound like a gunshot. Obie jumped, spilling his drink all over himself. Holding his hands over his ears, he ran into the station. I started to go after him, but the man in the white suit turned to me.

"What's wrong with your friend?" he asked.

"Nothin'," I said. "That noise surprised him, I guess."

Wiping his hands on a silk handkerchief, he introduced himself.

"I'm Brother Dwayne Goodall, and we're gonna have a revival here real soon. You ought to bring your friend out. We'll have preachin' and healin' and miracle workin'."

He didn't look like a preacher to me. He looked more like an actor. And I sure didn't know that preachers drove fancy cars. Our preacher, Reverend Allen, drove a beat-up old Ford.

"I don't know if Obie needs healin'," I said. Then, remembering my manners, I added, "Sir."

"There's something wrong with him, though, isn't there?" He said it kindly.

"Yessir, kind of," I said, choosing my words carefully.

"Well, then, sister," said Brother Goodall, "the boy needs healin'."

To tell the truth, I wasn't real sure what he meant by "healin'," but it sounded like something that maybe could do Obie some good. If Brother Goodall could fix Obie so that he didn't act up and do crazy things like pettin' snakes, then fine. I was pretty sure that healin' wasn't like miracle workin'. That was what God did. Maybe God worked miracles and Brother Goodall worked healin's.

"Well, I'll think about it," I said. "And thank you."

I went into the station to get Obie. He was curled up on the floor next to the Coke box, rocking back and forth.

"Obie," I said softly, "get up now."

He looked up at me like he didn't know me. But then he stopped rocking and got slowly to his feet. I turned to go, and he came up behind me and put his arms around my shoulders gently. He tried to hug me, but he was all sticky with strawberry drink. I pulled away. "Hey, let go!" I said, wriggling out of his grasp. "What's the matter with you anyway?"

Obie looked shocked. "You're mean!" he said, backing away.

"But Obie, look at you. You're a mess. Now go get cleaned up."

"I don't have to if I don't want to!" he said loudly.

That's when I left the station, without even

telling Bubba good-bye. I just felt worn out from all Obie's nonsense. Walking as fast as I could, I went toward the newspaper office, where I could see Armistead's truck parked out front.

Obie was right behind me. Outside the office, he spotted an empty pack of Lucky Strike cigarettes on the sidewalk. Before he could jump on it, I said, "At least give me the tinfoil first. *Then* jump on the pack three times. You'll still get good luck."

Obie practically threw the foil at me. I smoothed it out and put it in my pocket. When he started to jump I said as nice as I could, "Obie. If you're gonna be my friend, you can't be all over me. That's all. You understand?"

But he kept on jumping. Then he put his hands over his ears and screamed as loud as he could, "I DON'T HAVE TO IF I DON'T WANT TO!"

I couldn't believe it. Obie had never yelled at me in his life. Tears filled my eyes and I jerked open the door and stepped inside. Billy Malone, who helped Armistead put the paper together, was standing at the layout table, pasting up ads. Printer's ink stained the cuffs of his starched white shirt.

"Hidy, Tattnall," he said. "You been runnin'? It's too hot to run."

"No sir," I said, taking a deep breath.

"Your daddy's over at the courthouse. He said to tell you to wait here for him. He'll be back directly."

The door opened again and Obie came in. I turned my back on him.

"Billy, can I paste up an ad?" I asked quickly. "My hands are clean." I held them out for him to see.

"Sure. You can do the Leaf and Petal Florist." He looked at Obie. "How you, buster? How's your mama?"

Obie turned his head and didn't reply. He sat down on a stool at the counter where the paper was cut and pasted before going to the printer's. Directly in front of him were the glass dishes that held hot wax and thick glass rollers for pasting.

I got the florist's ad and, ignoring Obie, brought it over to the counter. I knew he was watching me. I ran the strip of paper carefully over the heavy roller so that it was sticky and ready for pasting, then turned to take it back to Billy.

Suddenly, there was a loud crash behind me. A roller had hit the floor hard, spattering hot wax everywhere.

Billy turned quickly. "You okay, Tattnall?" he asked. "You have to be careful, sugah. That stuff's hot! Obie, did any of it get on you?"

Obie started rocking, fast, his body shaking

the stool. I looked at him in disbelief. It was he—not me—who'd pushed that roller onto the floor. And he'd done it on purpose.

Angrily, I got down on the floor to clean up the mess. Just then the door breezed open and Miss Clarissa came in. She was all dressed up and smelled like carnations.

Obie stopped his rocking and went over to put his arms around his mama.

"I *thought* I'd find you all here," she said. "What's the matter, Obie?"

"Just a little accident with the wax," Billy answered for him. "No harm done."

"Are you all right?" she said, giving him a hug. "Well, we better get goin'. We've got errands to do."

Obie followed his mama to the door. As they walked out, Armistead arrived. "Ya'll leavin' us?" he asked, holding the door for them.

"I'm takin' Obie to the barbershop," said Miss Clarissa.

"Goin' to get yours ears lowered?" Armistead asked teasingly. But Obie wasn't in any mood for teasing. He just stomped on down the street, and Miss Clarissa hurried to catch up with him.

As he started to take off his seersucker jacket, Armistead saw me down on my knees smoothing wax onto the wooden floor.

"We just had a little spill," said Billy.

"*Obie* had a little spill," I mumbled.

"Come on, missy," Armistead said. "Let's go over to the cafe for lunch. Miss Ellie's got apple pie today."

When our order of fried chicken, mashed potatoes, black-eyed peas, corn bread, and apple pie had arrived, Armistead looked over at me. "Now, do you want to tell me what happened back at the office?" he asked.

"Nothin' much," I said.

"You mean to tell me you were down on your knees polishing floors 'cause you like it?" He shook his head. "Sugah, that dog won't hunt." He took a sip of iced tea.

"Armistead," I said with a sigh, "if you had to say something's wrong with Obie, what would you say it is?"

"Obie been givin' you trouble?"

"Kind of," I said. I told him about what happened at the filling station and how Obie yelled at me, then pushed the hot wax container onto the floor.

"I didn't actually *see* him push it," I said, putting my fork down. I didn't feel hungry. "He never used to be mean."

"Obie's not mean," said Armistead softly.

"He's . . . troubled, but not mean. He wouldn't hurt a living soul, especially you. He loves you."

"Well, he's got a funny way of showin' it," I said, wishing I could make Armistead understand.

Just then, Brother Goodall's big white car passed in front of the cafe. I figured it was a sign, and I should look toward it for a solution to Obie's problem. I made up my mind then and there that I was going to get Obie healed. If anybody could make him better, Jesus could. And maybe Brother Goodall could help.

When our waitress came by to refill our tea glasses, I said, "Can I have some ice cream on my pie, please?"

On Sunday afternoon, Bubba and I were sitting on the fence near the cattle gap.

"Guess what?" he said. "You remember that preacher at my pa's station?"

"I was gonna talk to you about him. What kind of preacher is he, anyway?"

"Daddy says he's an evangelist," said Bubba. "He travels everywhere preachin' revivals. Anyway, he came back by the station with a poster tellin' about one that's gonna be held tomorrow night and the next. They're putting up a tent in Mr. Roundtree's pasture."

"Bubba, I been thinkin' that maybe we could get Obie healed."

Bubba was quiet for a moment. Then he said, "You know somethin'? I been thinkin' about him too. I didn't want to say anything 'cause you get all upset if you think somebody's criticizing him. But he *is* acting funny lately. To tell you the truth, Tattnall, I don't much like bein' around him anymore." He looked over at me sideways to see how I'd take what he said. When I didn't say anything, he breathed a sigh of relief.

"It'll be hard gettin' Obie out there, though," he continued, jumping right to the practical, "what with Miss Clarissa not letting him out at night. But I believe we should take him. That preacher said he could heal him, right?"

"Kind of," I said, trying to remember just what he had said. "He said that Obie *needed* healing. And I figure that's the same thing."

As it turned out, sneaking away was easy. The first night of the revival was scheduled for the same night as the bond rally downtown. Everybody in Pinella was working hard to support the war effort and they were all going to the rally, including my folks.

"They'll be gone most of the evening," I told Bubba as we sat on the back stoop making our plans. "I told them that we didn't want to go, because we wanted to hear *The Shadow* on the radio. That it was the second of a two-parter and we had to find out how it was going to end."

"That might work," Bubba said. "There's just one problem." He reached down and started untying, then tying, his shoelaces.

"What?" I asked.

"Zinnia wants to go with us."

"Oh, shoot, Bubba. Why'd you tell her about it? You know she'll blab."

"I had to," he said. "I'm supposed to be taking care of her."

"So help me, if she tells . . ."

"She won't," said Bubba. "I know she won't."

Just before Armistead and Grandmother went to get Miss Clarissa, Grandmother issued a warning:

"You and Obie can stay here and listen to your radio program since it seems to be so important to you. And if Bubba and Zinnia want to come over, that's fine. But there's to be *no* monkey business. There's lemonade in the icebox and Virgie's left you some cake and . . ." She stopped. "You all behave yourselves, you hear me?"

CHAPTER 10

"How much farther?" asked Zinnia, taking off her shoes and walking barefoot in the soft, fine dust of the road.

"It's not far now," said Bubba, "and quit complainin'. You wanted to come."

What a pain she is, I thought, but I didn't say anything. It was too early in the evening to bother with Zinnia. Besides, I had to take care of Obie. He wasn't too happy 'cause we told him Icarus couldn't come with us, that we didn't think dogs were allowed at revivals. I was just praying that he'd behave. When I first told him where we were going, all he said was, "I'm gonna wear my sweater."

"Yeah, okay. But Obie, listen to me. Will you please try and *concentrate* when the preacher talks to you?" I wasn't sure what would happen but I thought it might be like a test.

"Whatever you say, I'll do," he answered obligingly.

"There," said Bubba, pointing to the top of the tent, which was barely visible through the trees.

It was set up in a field that was now thick with cars, trucks, and wagons. Small children and a few dogs were running around. When Obie saw the dogs, he opened his mouth to protest.

"Now, Obie," I said. "This is like church. You couldn't take Icarus inside, any more than you can on Sunday. Here, hold still for a minute—let me smooth down your hair." I didn't even bother about his tie. "Now, we don't have to stay for the whole thing, just the healin' part." As I explained to him again about why we'd come, he held tightly to my hand, soaking up all the attention I was giving him.

Inside the big tent, there was a sense of excitement. Some people were seated on hard wooden benches and others sat on folding chairs. The ground was covered with sweet-smelling wood shavings, and lanterns hung high in the shadows. Footlights lit up the wooden platform, where several men were seated in tall chairs. The only one I recognized was Brother Goodall. At his right, near the edge of the platform, a lady was playing an upright piano.

"I didn't know it would be so crowded," Bubba said as we finally found four seats together.

"Yeah, there's more sinners in town than I thought," I said, picking up a cardboard fan from the seat of my chair. On one side was a picture of a bunch of children lined up to talk to Jesus, and printed on the back was the name of the undertaker in Pinella.

Zinnia was standing up on her chair, looking to see if anybody she knew was there. But the more I looked around, the more I thought that maybe coming hadn't been such a good idea after all. I punched Bubba on the arm.

"I think we ought to leave," I said. "I didn't figure on so many folks being here."

Bubba glanced around and nodded. He pulled on Zinnia's skirt, and when she sat down he whispered to her. Zinnia shook her head emphatically. "I am *not* leavin'!" she said loudly. "I want to hear the songs and see somebody get healed."

Obie was looking straight ahead, but the back of his neck seemed stiff, like he couldn't move it. Reaching across Bubba, I pinched Zinnia's arm as hard as I could. "Come *on,* Zinnia! Right now!"

Zinnia yelped. "You're the biggest sinner out here, Tattnall Holcomb! You ought to stay for sure!"

Just then, Brother Goodall signaled to the piano player. The chords of "Onward, Christian Soldiers!" resounded through the tent with the fury of crashing cymbals. People began clapping in time to the music. There was a sense of electricity in the air, the way the earth feels just before a storm. Brother Goodall jumped to his feet like a rocket, his white suit gleaming in the footlights. He walked to the edge of the platform and looked out into the audience.

"The prophet Isaiah has spoken!" he shouted. "We are a sinful nation, a people laden with iniquity, a seed of evildoers! Children that are corrupters; they have forsaken the Lord!"

He was looking straight at me when he said that about evildoers. Then, in a voice that sounded like doom, he said, "Wash you, make you clean; put away the evil of your doings from before mine eyes; cease to do evil."

Bubba reached out and took my hand and I took Obie's. Then Brother Goodall said some more Bible verses about sin and the clefts of rocks and stuff. The louder he shouted, the more excited the people became. There was clapping and stomping and lots of shouted "Amens!"

Suddenly, Brother Goodall turned, bent his body from the waist, and stomped across the stage. "I was driving through your county and the Holy Spirit gave me a message! There's sinners here that need to repent! Ordinary Christians who need saving. And I'm here to tell you, I'm gonna save 'em!" His head whipped around in all directions, as if it was on a swivel. And his eyes kept coming back to us, time after time.

The tent was hot as blazes and Brother Goodall's words rose to the top like steam rising from a kettle. The noise grew and swelled. All of a sudden, the lady at the piano slammed down on the keys so hard it's a wonder the wires didn't snap. She played for a few minutes, then stopped. There was a silence. Then Brother Goodall shattered it with a sermon that was filled with enough fire and brimstone that you could smell sulfur.

"God is angry with great numbers that are now on earth; yea, and with many who are now in this congregation! The devil stands ready to fall upon them, and seize them as his own. They belong to him!" A woman in the back row began sobbing. Obie's eyes were round as plates and Bubba hadn't moved a muscle since the sermon began.

"The old serpent is gaping for them! *Hell* opens its mouth wide to receive them! Consider the fearful danger you are in; it is a great furnace of wrath, a wide and bottomless pit, and you hang by only a slender thread."

By the time the sermon ended, my knees had turned to rubber and I could feel the flames of hell licking around my feet. The lady at the piano began playing and folks in the audience started moving down the aisles toward the front. Two of the men on the platform with Brother Goodall rose and moved forward, holding what looked like big white napkins in their hands.

A lady approached the platform and stood in front of Brother Goodall. He leaned in close to her and said something in a low voice, then cried out, "Heal this sinner!" He smacked her forehead with the palm of his hand and she dropped to her knees, then fell on the floor like she'd been struck by lightning. One of the men placed a big cloth over her knees to cover them.

"Bubba, now we've really got to leave," I said. "I didn't tell Obie anything about getting hit. I didn't know about it."

The music was soft now, an old hymn that seemed to float on the air. Standing in front of his chair, Obie started to sing, his voice ringing out pure and sweet.

"Amazing grace, how sweet the sound,
That saved a wretch like me,
I once was lost, but now am found,
Was blind, but now I see."

And an odd thing happened. Everyone else stopped singing. Obie stood alone in the dim light singing "Amazing Grace" as if he had just plucked it out of the air. When he finished, some of the ladies were crying. Then, a man came up from behind us and began to pound Obie on the back, saying how wonderful it was that this sinner was going to be saved. And the next thing I knew, he'd taken Obie by the hand and was leading him straight up to the front of the tent.

The singing and clapping grew louder. Obie was up on the platform surrounded by strangers. Even if he hadn't been wearing his red sweater in the summertime, he'd have stood out in a crowd. His cowlick was standing straight up on his head and there was a look of abject fear on his face. In the midst of all those people, he seemed alone and lost. He was squinting in the light and searching the crowd and I knew he was looking for me to come rescue him.

The excitement of the revival was swelling. Some folks were crying in their exaltation, while others raised their arms up into the air and shouted. One woman began speaking in tongues.

Brother Goodall was standing directly in front of Obie. Suddenly, he smacked Obie's forehead. "Heal this sinner!" he said. "Heal!"

Obie looked like he'd been turned to stone, like all the breath had been knocked out of him. I tasted the salt of my tears.

Zinnia was standing up on her chair, her eyes bright with excitement.

"That's enough!" she announced. "I'm gonna go get him. I don't think he likes it up there." And before I could even think straight, she began pushing and shoving her way to the platform. She walked right up to a man who was leading Obie off to the side, and with the strength of the righteous, took Obie's hand and led him back through the crowd and out into the gentleness of the summer night.

It was a sad-looking group that walked back down the dusty road toward home. Bubba, Zinnia, and Obie walked in front of me, Bubba kicking the powdery dust with his bare feet. He'd taken his shoes off and tied them around his neck by their laces. Obie hadn't said a single, solitary word since being "healed." I was afraid he'd been struck dumb, like Lot's wife. The hum of katydids rose and fell and the music from the tent drifted faintly over the fields.

Several cars passed us as folks left the revival. We'd moved over to the side of the road when a black Buick, big as a hearse, slowed, then stopped in front of us.

"Is that Tattnall Holcomb?"

"Oh, lordy," I whispered to Bubba, "I believe that's Billy Malone. Sure as guns're iron he's gonna tell Armistead he saw us out here." Walking slowly over to the car, I looked in the window. "Yessir," I said, as polite as I could be.

"You all want a ride?" Billy asked. "You shouldn't be out here at dark."

"No sir," I said. "But thank you anyway." He drove off and we watched till we couldn't see the taillights of the car.

We walked on for a little while, then Bubba said, "I sure hope Mama ain't home yet. 'Cause if she is, she's gonna skin me alive."

"Yeah," piped up Zinnia, "and Daddy's gonna be mad 'cause you made me come along."

"Aw, shut up, Zinnia," he said. "I told you not to come but you wouldn't listen."

"Well," she said righteously, "if I hadn't, who would have helped Obie? Who? That's what I want to know."

Even though I knew I was going to hear about

it for the rest of my natural-born life, Zinnia was right. I had failed Obie when he needed me. She'd taken care of him when I couldn't.

"Zinnia?" said Obie, his voice startling in the darkness. "Did I get healed?"

"Sure you did," she said firmly. "Good as anybody."

We stopped at the foot of the drive. All the lights were on and the pickup truck was parked at the side. And what was worse, Billy's car was there too, lookin' black as death.

"Looks like we're in trouble," said Bubba.

"Looks like it," I said. "Obie, I'm really sorry I let you down like that. I sure didn't mean to hurt you."

Obie smiled, his face pale in the starlight. "It's okay, Tattnall," he said.

I looked at him, at the way his shoulder blades stuck out like wings and how his tie was all crooked. "Oh, I just wish you'd get mad at me or something."

Bubba and Zinnia started down the road. "Bubba," I said, "you want me to ask my daddy to drive ya'll home?"

He shook his head. "No, thanks, we'll get there soon enough, I reckon."

"Well, *I* want a ride," said Zinnia. "I'm tired."

"Let's go, Zinnia," said Bubba.

As Obie and I walked up the drive, he took my hand. Suddenly, he began to sing:

"... how sweet the sound
That saved a wretch like me ..."

The words just about broke my heart. "Don't sing, Obie," I said. "I just can't stand it if you sing."

CHAPTER 11

"I wish everybody'd just sue me and get it over with," I said over my shoulder.

I was sitting on the back steps. The screened door was open and I could hear Virgie and Grandmother working in the kitchen. They were making pickled peaches while the day was halfway cool.

"Everything stinks," I grumbled.

"That's vinegar you smell," said Grandmother, coming over to the back door. "And for heaven's sake, Tattnall, hush. You've been sitting out there all morning, and you've been *complainin'* all morning. I wish you'd find something to do."

"There's nothing *to* do," I said. "I'm not

allowed to do anything." Looking down at my bare feet, I decided that my right big toe looked just like Lou Costello.

"You could repent your sins," said Virgie, speaking to me for the first time that day.

Truth was, everybody was mad at me, not only for running off to the revival but mostly for not telling the truth. At first, Virgie wouldn't even speak to me, she was so mad. Grandmother said she was too old to put up with that kind of nonsense, and Armistead said that if I was twins he'd be in the loony bin.

That night, when Obie and I had walked up to the house, Billy Malone was coming out my front door. When he saw me, he came over, and nice as anything said, "Well, sugah, you had your daddy scared pretty good. But I told him I'd seen you coming back from the revival meeting and that you all were safe and sound."

In one second flat, my stomach fell to my knees. But all I said was, "Thanks, Billy."

Armistead and Grandmother were waiting for us in the hall, and what was worse, Miss Clarissa was in the living room, just sitting there like a big old spider. When we walked in, Armistead marched us directly in there. Miss Clarissa stood up. First, she went over to Obie and checked him out to be sure he was fine. She acted like I'd kidnapped him or something. Then she hopped on me like a duck on a june bug.

"Tattnall Holcomb," she said, her voice trembling. "This time you have really done it. You have gone too far, missy. And I've had enough."

"But Miss Clarissa," I said, "it's okay. Honest. Obie got healed but I don't think it took. He just sang and got taken up on the stage."

Well, *that* was sure the wrong thing to say. Miss Clarissa looked like she was gonna pass out. "Up on the stage!" She turned to Armistead. "Did you hear that? Up on the stage? You'd best do something about this child before she turns into a criminal. She's already a juvenile delinquent!"

"The man didn't hit me hard," Obie said.

Miss Clarissa stared at him, her mouth open.

"Lord, have mercy on us," she said. "Mama! Did you hear that? Did you? It's worse than I thought."

"Now, sister," Armistead said. "That's enough. The children didn't do anything so terrible. They went to a revival. They didn't rob the bank."

"We're going home now," said Miss Clarissa, gathering up her purse and some bags of stuff from the rally. "I'd appreciate it if you'd give us a ride, Armistead. It's the last thing I'll ever ask!"

The upshot was that Obie had to stay in his

house, Bubba got a whipping and was grounded, and I was just grounded. Lucky for me, Armistead didn't believe in whippings. Of course, nothin' happened to Zinnia. She weaseled her way out of everything, like she always did.

Later on that night, when Armistead and I were sitting on the screened porch, I asked him, "Are you all mad 'cause I left Obie up on the stage and Zinnia had to go get him?"

White moths hit the screens with soft plops.

"Obie's the only one who should be angry about that," he said. "No, I'm upset because you sneaked around to do something you knew was wrong." He paused a moment. "And from now on, *think* before you act, darlin'. Think about how your actions will reflect on someone else, particularly when that someone is as vulnerable as Obie."

"I didn't mean to hurt him. I care more about him than almost anybody, but . . ."

"What?"

I took a deep breath. "Sometimes I just get tired of lookin' after him. I mean, I'm not his mama, although everybody seems to forget that. And Obie can't do the things I want to do." I wasn't exactly sure what those things were, but I knew I wanted to do them without Obie.

"Is that why you took him out to the revival?

To help him? Is that what you thought 'healing' would do?"

"I guess so," I said. "But I didn't really believe it."

"Tattnall, none of us adults expects you to watch out for Obie all the time. We understand you have a life of your own."

"Miss Clarissa doesn't think so," I said. "Besides, if I'm not looking after him, he gets in trouble and he gets mad at me. Lately, he can be really mean. It's a fact, whether anyone believes me or not." And for emphasis, I got straight up and went into the house.

Finally, everybody got over being mad. Even Miss Clarissa, who'd threatened to put my picture in the post office under the "Most Wanted" list, started speaking again, although she didn't have much to say to me. Bubba was allowed to leave his house without Zinnia. Being with her all the time was too much punishment for anyone, I thought.

"Heckfire," I'd told Virgie, "I bet we could send Zinnia overseas as a secret weapon."

"Do, chile," she said, shaking her head.

Whip-poor-will . . . whip-poor-will . . . The plaintive notes sounded just outside my window. I hoped the pesky thing wouldn't call all night; sometimes, they just call and call, over and over again, like a broken record. Then, bits of gravel sprayed the screen. I turned down the page in my book to save my place and went over to the window. Obie was standing out in the bright moonlight. I slipped down the stairs and went outside to meet him.

"I'm running away," he said.

"Where to?"

He shrugged. "The cemetery. To one of those little houses."

For a moment, I couldn't think what he meant. Then I said, "Oh, Obie, those aren't little houses. They're tombs. You can't live there. Dead people are in there."

He stood in front of me, rocking from side to side.

"Why do you want to run away?" I asked.

He shrugged. " 'Cause," he said.

"Listen, Miss Clarissa can't keep you inside all the time. She'll get over it. Besides, if you ran away she'd come looking for you."

"I'll join the navy," he said.

"Obie, come on now." I felt myself getting impatient with him. "Anyway, you can't run away without any money."

"You can give me some," he said. "We could

take all your money and ride the train somewhere."

"That's impossible."

Obie's face twisted like he was going to cry. "Why won't you?" he asked. He put his hands out in front of him like he was blind and reaching for something. "Why won't you?"

I knew then for sure that the healing hadn't done a thing, that it had all been for nothing. "Please, Obie. Just go on home now, you hear me?" My feet were soaking wet from the dew and I wanted to go inside.

He looked hard at me, his eyes searching my face as though he wanted to understand but couldn't. Then he turned abruptly and started back across the moon-spattered lawn, Icarus following close on his heels. I hurried after him. "Obie," I said, trying to take his arm. But he pulled away, and I knew I'd hurt his feelings again.

CHAPTER 12

Grandmother removed the last straight pin from the hem of the crisp, dotted-swiss dress and stood up. My twelfth birthday was just three days away, and she was making me a dress for the occasion. "Now turn around slowly," she said.

Satisfied that the hem was even, she carefully slipped the dress over my head. The material smelled sweet, and was the color of ripe cherries. "I've had that piece of goods since before the war," she said, smoothing it with her hands. "It came all the way from Belgium."

I looked at myself in her long mirror. "I hate my hair," I said. "I just *hate* it." Claire had given me a home permanent and it had frizzed. And I was getting so tall that I just knew I'd tower over everyone else in my class. "I look like a giraffe with frizzy hair!"

"Oh, for heaven's sake, Tattnall," said Grandmother, taking my dress over to the ironing board. "It'll fall."

"I hope it falls *out*!" I mourned. "And before my birthday!"

"What do you want for your birthday, anyway?" Claire asked, coming into the room with a stack of patterns to show Grandmother.

"A charm bracelet like yours and a diary with a lock and key," I replied.

"Who'd you invite to your party?" she asked.

"Ruth Anne Ramsey from school, Bubba, Zinnia, and Obie," I replied. I didn't have many friends close by. Since we lived out in the country, it was hard for other kids to come see me. But Ruth Anne had persuaded her mother to drive her, and I was kind of excited about her coming.

"I'm sorry I won't be here," Claire said, picking up a brush from the dresser and sitting down next to me on the bed. "But I have to go to Selma." She was working on an article about women doing war work, and interviewing some ladies about their jobs. "Now be still," she added, attacking some of my curls.

"It's okay," I said. "Ouch, Claire! That's a tangle, not a curl."

"Hey, how would you like it if I took you and your friends up to the dam for a picnic?"

I was really surprised. I couldn't believe that she'd actually take me and my friends anywhere. "I've never been to the dam," I said.

"Well, it's not much, but it's the biggest thing around Pinella."

So we just moved my birthday party up a day. My friends were invited to a picnic, then we'd come back home for ice cream and cake.

I was surprised that Obie decided to come to my party. He'd been staying away from me since the night he'd talked about running away. But now here he was, all dressed up except for his sweater, and holding tight to my present. Virgie told me that Miss Clarissa said he couldn't come if he wore that "smelly old thing." She said she was sick of looking at it and she was taking it to the cleaners.

"And no dogs!" Claire stated as we all climbed into the truck. I could tell Obie was upset about that, and wanted me to talk to him, but I was too busy. It was the first time Ruth Anne had been to my house and I had to be polite to her.

From where Claire parked the truck to the top of the dam was a pretty good climb. She led the way, her white blouse gleaming in the dense shade. She'd brought a camera so that she could take pictures to send to Ted. All the way up the hill, Zinnia kept posing beside sassafras bushes saying, "How's this look? This would be a good picture."

Ruth Anne and I walked together, carrying the picnic basket between us. Obie was directly ahead.

"What's the matter with your friend?" Ruth Anne asked, loudly enough for him to hear. I didn't know what to say. At first I acted like I didn't hear her. But then she turned and looked straight at me, so I had to say something.

"He's not really my friend, he's sort of my cousin," I mumbled. A wave of guilt washed over me as Obie glanced back at us, then stumbled on the path. But before I could say anything else, he'd zoomed off, his arms spread wide.

"Hey, look at him go!" Ruth Anne laughed. And I laughed too.

At last, we found a level spot overlooking the river, where we spread the quilts we'd brought. Nearby, we discovered a small pond where pink lotus flowers grew. Claire took a picture of Zinnia holding a flower, then said, "Okay. Now, everybody get in this one." Bubba and Ruth Anne and I moved to the edge of the pond behind Zinnia. Claire focused the camera. "Where's Obie?" she said. "I want him in this, too."

"I thought he was right behind me," said Bubba.

"Must've just zoomed off," Ruth Anne said, giggling.

Bubba looked disgusted, and moved away from us. He didn't like people making fun of Obie any more than I did—usually. But here I was, hurting Obie's feelings because I wanted to make Ruth Anne like me. All of a sudden, I was sorry I'd even invited her to my party.

We all started calling, "Obieee . . . Obieee . . . Where are you?"

But there was no answer. He'd just disappeared. "Let's separate and go look for him," said Bubba.

"No," said Claire. "If we all go running off, we'll just lose each other.

Below us, the river gleamed and glittered. We started walking, keeping to the river's edge, all the time calling, "Obieee . . . Obie . . . Obie . . ."

Then I saw him: a lone figure standing on the jetty that jutted out into the water.

"Claire?" I said softly, pointing in his direction.

We all stood stricken, looking out toward the river.

"Oh, my Lord," breathed Claire.

We began running down the bank, trying to get closer to Obie. When we got to the land's end, Obie turned and saw us. He was barely balancing on the narrow strip, moving like someone on a tightrope.

"Obie!" Claire yelled. "Get yourself back here this minute. You hear me?"

Obie kind of jumped up and down, laughing to beat the band.

"He's gonna fall in," said Bubba fearfully. "And he can't swim a stroke."

Ruth Anne was standing next to me, biting her nails. Her curly red hair was a blaze in the summer sun. "What's he gonna do?" she asked.

I was so scared I couldn't talk. I felt like there was a lump in my throat that held the words back. Claire started down the slope. "I'm going after him," she said. "And when I get him, I'm going to strangle him."

"There's not enough room for both of you on that thing," I said, the words coming out in a rush. "Obie!" I yelled. "We haven't had our picnic yet. Come on back. You can cut the cake, okay?"

Zinnia yelled out, "If you don't get back here right now, we're gonna eat the picnic and not save any for you!"

He turned his back on us.

By this time, Claire was at the foot of the jetty. She slipped off her tennis shoes and moved slowly and carefully down its length. As she drew closer, Obie walked farther out, one step at a time, putting one foot in front of the other. When he reached the end, he stopped, and then, balancing on one foot, began to take off his trousers. When he was done, he stood on the jetty in his white underwear, his skinny legs wobbling back and forth.

Claire moved steadily closer. He stood perfectly still, watching her. As she began to reach out for him, he waved his trousers over his head like a flag and shouted, "God bless America and all the ships at sea!" Then he jumped into the deep, deep water.

Without a moment's hesitation, Claire dove in after him, her slim form as swift and sure as an arrow. I watched as she swam through the current. *Please, please let them be all right. Oh, please,* I said over and over inside my head. I could hear Bubba's breathing in the quiet.

"Gosh," said Zinnia in awe. "She looks just like Esther Williams!"

Claire cut through the water with clean, strong strokes. She caught Obie and towed him back to shore, her arm close around his neck. We all helped drag him up onto the bank and a few minutes later, we had him wrapped in a quilt, sitting in the cab of the truck.

"He's a lucky boy," Armistead said later as we sat on the porch eating my birthday cake. "He jumped on the side of the jetty away from the dam," he explained to Grandmother. "Otherwise, Claire wouldn't have been able to find him and fight the swift current, too. She saved his life."

"Dear Lord," Grandmother said softly.

But of course, it wasn't as easy as all that. What had happened was my fault, even if no one else knew it.

Miss Clarissa nearly had a stroke when she found out what Obie'd done, but she didn't say a word to me about it. Ruth Anne's mama called that evening to say that she didn't think it a good idea for Ruth Anne to come play if Obie was going to be around.

The next day, on my real birthday, Armistead gave me a charm bracelet and Claire gave me a diary, with a lock and key. I took some birthday cake straight over to Obie, anxious to apologize for what he'd overheard. But Miss Clarissa just thanked me curtly and said that Obie was a little "under the weather" and couldn't come downstairs.

"Virgie," I said, moving the stack of freshly ironed pillowcases from the window seat so I could sit down, "do you think Obie remembers things the way other people do?"

She glanced at me suspiciously. We were in the

little room at the top of the stairs, where she was ironing. Picking up the Coca-Cola bottle with a stopper in it, she sprinkled the sleeves of her choir robe. "I can't say for certain. Why? You do something to Obie you'd just as soon he forget?" she asked. Steam rose from the crisp white cotton, filling the room with the scent of starch and linen.

"No," I said quickly. "Well, sort of."

"I knew it," Virgie said. "You and Miss Nasty-Nice been pickin' on him."

"You mean Ruth Anne?"

"Huummph," she said, thumping down hard with the iron.

I told her what had happened. And how I'd hurt Obie's feelings. "That's why he jumped in the river," I said. "It was my fault."

Virgie stopped ironing. She picked up her glass of iced tea, which was beaded with moisture, and held it up to cool her forehead. "Obie reminds me of a rabbit I saw once in the woods. It was caught in a trap. I quick ran and got Enoch and he came and freed it."

"Then what happened?" I asked.

"It had to be put down," she said. "It was too hurt to live."

Something gripped my heart. All of a sudden, the room was stifling and I had trouble catching my breath.

CHAPTER 13

"I am sick and tired of Roy Rogers and Trigger," I said. "Besides, this whole puzzle's brown and white. Let's quit."

"Suits me," said Bubba, pushing away from the card table we'd set up on the screened porch. His folks had dropped him off on their way to Selma to have Zinnia's eyes tested, and he'd brought the puzzle with him.

"Want to go see if Obie can come over?" I said, still wanting to apologize to him.

"Suits me," Bubba repeated.

Armistead came out to the porch. He was wearing his old straw hat and had a notepad in his breast pocket.

"I've got some serious business to take care of," he said. "Ya'll want to come with me?"

"We were on our way to Obie's."

"He can come too," Armistead said excitedly. "Come to think of it, he *should* come too." Without any further explanation, he headed out to the truck, with us following behind.

On our way to Obie's house, he told us what was going on. "We're going to meet a real, live hero. One of America's first fighter pilot Aces." He explained that Michael McIntosh, whose daddy owned a plantation out on the edge of town, had returned to the States after flying with General Chennault's American Volunteer Group. "He'll only be here for a day or so before he joins the U.S. Marine Black Sheep Squadron, and he's agreed to let me interview him for the paper."

"Holy smoke!" said Bubba. He reached over to Armistead and held out his hand. "I surely do appreciate this, sir," he said.

Obie and Icarus climbed into the back of the truck with Bubba. Before I had a chance to say anything, Obie touched my shoulder gently, and I knew he'd either forgotten or forgiven me for what had happened with Ruth Anne.

"Hurry!" I said to Armistead, suddenly light-headed with excitement.

"Beg your pardon?"

"Please, I mean. He might not wait!"

By the time we reached the McIntosh plantation, several trucks were already there, parked haphazardly under the trees near the fence. Nearby, a group of men were clustered around a tall, thin man wearing a white shirt and khaki pants.

"Is that him?" I asked, as we climbed out of the truck. I kind of figured he'd be wearing a uniform, a leather jacket like the men in the movie *Flying Tigers*.

"That's him," said Armistead. "Now, after I introduce you all, I expect you to make yourselves scarce for a while. I've got business to take care of." He looked at Obie. "And son, I expect you to behave. No funny business."

"I won't," said Obie. "I mean, I will."

We stood in line to greet Michael McIntosh. He was really handsome, like a movie star. I wished that I had worn my new dress that made me look older. When it was Obie's turn to shake hands, he was so awed that he could barely meet the flier's eyes.

"I understand from Mr. Holcomb that you're a real fan," said Michael, smiling. His eyes were as gray as fog. Obie nodded. "And that you know a lot about planes." Again, Obie nodded. "Well, I'm glad to have you on our side."

Obie just stood there, unable to speak. "C'mon," I said, taking his hand and leading him away. "Let's go see the plane."

Obie buzzed across the field to the pasture, his arms held out as he swooped and turned. The plane sat at the far end of the pasture, its wings shining in the sunlight. On the fuselage, the shark face grinned whitely, its painted eye sinister.

The minute he saw it, Obie stopped flying and walked slowly toward it.

"Gee whiz!" said Bubba admiringly. "That's the best-lookin' hunk of metal I ever saw!"

Obie walked all the way around the plane. He laid his hands flat against the warm metal as though he could feel some vibration from where it had been. He touched the number written on the side. Then he headed for the fuselage. Reaching up, he ran his fingers over the painted face as delicately as someone reading Braille.

"Obie?" I said, standing near the wheels, which smelled hot in the sun.

He looked at me and smiled, his face alight with joy.

A little while later, Bubba and I started back across the pasture. "What's wrong?" Bubba asked.

"Nothin'," I said.

"Then why are you cryin'?" he asked.

I shook my head and turned to see if Obie was following us. But he and Icarus were both still next to the plane, in the shadow of the wings. When Obie saw me looking at him, he raised his hand in a kind of salute. Then, calmly picking up Icarus, he climbed onto the wing.

"Bubba," I said, grabbing his arm, barely able to speak. He turned to look back just as Obie slipped into the cockpit.

"Oh, my gosh!" he said. We started running toward the plane, and behind us Armistead gave a shout.

"Obie!" I yelled.

"Stop!" cried Bubba.

The engines started with a little cough, then the propellers caught the sun in their blades and sparked silver. Slowly, the plane taxied across the field, gradually building speed. The sound of the engine grew louder. Cows in the adjoining field began scattering in all directions, *thumpety . . . thump . . . thump*, the sound of their hooves mingling with the sound of men running over the ground.

The plane slowed, made a graceful right turn, and skirted the pond as cleanly as a sailboat tacks into the wind. It was headed directly for the giant oak in the middle of the pasture. Suddenly, the engine sputtered, then quit. The plane came to rest inches away from the tree. When the engine died, it seemed like all sound had been sucked out of the air.

A moment later, Obie pushed back the plane's canopy. With Icarus in his arms, he climbed down the wing and jumped onto the ground. Behind us, Armistead said softly, "Lord, have mercy on us."

The men began to move about, watching as Obie walked across the pasture, his dog in his arms. When he realized that people were looking at him, he put Icarus down and just stood, a lone figure outlined by the sun.

And then Michael McIntosh did something stunning. It was a gesture that folks in Pinella talked about for a long time afterward. Leaving the others, he walked across that field to where Obie stood with only Icarus for company. When he got close, he held out his hand.

"Let's take a ride, son," he said. "We'll take her up."

Then, waving to the group of shocked bystanders, the fighter pilot Ace, Michael McIntosh, took Obie up into the clouds.

CHAPTER 14

There was a signed photograph of the Flying Tigers on the wall in Armistead's office. Across it, Michael McIntosh had written:

> Born of the sun they traveled a short while
> towards the sun,
> And left the vivid air signed with their honor.
> —Stephen Spender

"Is Stephen Spender an Ace, too?" I asked, admiring the picture of the planes, flying high in the air.

"No," said Armistead, "he's a poet. A very fine one."

• • •

Overnight, the weather turned crisp and cool. Piles of bright orange pumpkins were offered for sale in vacant lots, while tall purple stalks of sugarcane leaned against the produce shelves of the grocery store. On Sunday evening, Grandmother, Armistead, and I were in the living room listening to *The Jack Benny Show* on the radio. The door was open to the screened porch and Lucky was lying on his back in the doorway between the two rooms.

"Yoo-hoo!" came a fluting call from outside.

Grandmother got up and went to the side door. "Clarissa? My goodness, darlin', you look like a ghost in this light. Come on in."

But Miss Clarissa took a seat on the porch and a minute later called Armistead to come out too.

"Why didn't you call me to come get you?" he said as he went out the door. "You don't need to be walking down the road this time of evenin'. Where's Obie?"

"In bed asleep," Miss Clarissa replied. "He's still worn out from all the excitement." She sighed, then said, "Actually, he's the reason I'm here. I've made a decision and I wanted you all to know about it."

The glider creaked as Armistead sat down. "I believe it's time for Obie to go off to Birmingham," she went on. Her voice sounded thick and soft, as though she'd been holding back the words that now came tumbling out in a rush. "He needs to go. He needs some help. I've talked to the people at St. John's School and they're very nice. It's a good place."

I kept very still, quietly turning the volume down on the radio. I wasn't sure I was supposed to be hearing this conversation.

"I haven't wanted to face this," she said, "but now I have to. Something's got to be done about my child."

"Oh, darlin'," said Grandmother, her voice as gentle as spring rain.

"Too many things have happened to him lately," said Miss Clarissa. She blew her nose. "I'm afraid for him these days. He's not the same, somehow. I know you all don't believe it, but I do realize that he's growing up. Maybe if his daddy hadn't died . . . I just don't know how to handle him anymore."

I couldn't listen any longer. "C'mon, Lucky," I said. We slipped out of the front door and went to the garden. Cool, dewy grass soaked my sneakers as I walked across the lawn. A sickle moon seemed caught at the very top of the magnolia tree and the evening star hung at its tip. I made a wish—a wish for Obie.

Inside, the table lamp on the screened porch came on, and I could see Grandmother's profile. She was leaning toward Miss Clarissa like she was listening real hard to what she was saying. Maybe she could talk her out of this. "It's not right," I whispered to Lucky, who responded by nuzzling my hand with his moist nose.

The tears started and I brushed them away angrily. I wondered if Miss Clarissa had told him he was going away. I should have stayed inside to try and convince her that this was a bad idea. What Obie needed was some room, but now Miss Clarissa was putting him in a place where they'd keep him. Even I knew that wasn't the right thing.

I didn't know what the right thing was, though.

That night, Armistead told me about Obie's going away to school. I didn't tell him I'd been eavesdropping.

"Does he know?" I asked.

"He knows, but I don't know how much he understands," he said, kissing me good night.

The next day, I decided to go see Obie. I took him some bubble gum and a new Captain Marvel comic book. He loved Captain Marvel, I guess 'cause he could fly.

Miss Clarissa came to the door.

"I brought Obie some stuff," I said.

At first I didn't think she was going to let me in. Then she said, "That's very thoughtful of you, Tattnall." She opened the screened door and I went into the hall. "Obie's in his room. Just go on up."

As I started up the stairs, she said, "Tattnall?"

"Yes, ma'am?"

"You've been mighty sweet to my boy. I'm sorry I never told you that before." Her face crumpled like tissue paper and I was scared she was going to cry.

I didn't know what to say. "I'll just go on up now," I replied lamely. Then she turned and walked back down the hall.

Obie was sitting on the edge of his bed, just staring into space. I gave him the comic book and bubble gum. "Are you excited about going to Birmingham?" I asked. But he was looking at Captain Marvel and didn't answer.

"Obie?" I said. "You can tell me. Why'd you try to fly that plane?"

He shook his head and almost smiled. "I scared you, didn't I?"

"Doggone it, Obie! You know you did. Now, listen to me for a minute. Put the funny book down."

He looked straight at me, and his expression

was so sad it just about broke my heart. "Obie, you've always been my best friend, even if I haven't always acted that way. You won't forget me, will you?"

"I hope the train goes too fast" was all he said.

There wasn't any passenger service from Pinella, so Armistead had to drive Obie and Miss Clarissa to Montgomery to catch the train to Birmingham. On the morning we left, Armistead took his old straw hat from the hall tree.

"When this war is over," Grandmother said, standing by the door, "I'm going to Tuscaloosa to buy you a new Panama straw hat."

"Nothin' wrong with this one, Mama," he said, the brim so soft and worn that it flopped down over his eyes.

"My dear," she said, and the tears in her eyes had nothing to do with his hat.

In the station, sunlight filtered through the glass-paned roof and there was a smell of oil and wood and dust. Servicemen slept on hard benches or played cards while they waited for their trains. At the newsstand, Armistead bought copies of the *Saturday Evening Post* and *Woman's Home Companion* for Miss Clarissa to read on the trip. Steam rose from the tracks of the waiting trains while redcaps, their carts filled with luggage, passed through the crowds of passengers.

Obie's train was called over the loudspeaker.

"Is that us?" asked Miss Clarissa, gathering her things around her like a broody hen with chicks. Picking up her flowered carryall, Armistead handed her the tickets, and we walked down the side of the train toward the car they were to board. Obie was looking all around, trying to see everything at once.

We got on the train with them and after Armistead found their seats and stowed Miss Clarissa's packages away, he asked the conductor to please look after them.

"Obie," I said, handing him the parcel wrapped with string, "I've got a present for you. It's Virgie's peanut brittle and a *Superman* comic book."

"Thank you," he said politely, putting the package on top of Ted's sweater, which was folded on the seat next to him. "I'll save it till tomorrow, when I come back."

"Oh, Obie," I said. "Maybe not tomorrow." Then, reaching up, I kissed his cheek, which felt cold to my touch. Awkwardly, he kissed me back, his lips missing my cheek and landing somewhere near my ear.

Then it was time for us to get off the train.

"I'll miss you, Obie," I said over my shoulder as I followed Armistead down the aisle.

"BOOOOAARRRD!" called the conductor. "ALL ABOOOAAARRRD!"

The train pulled slowly out of the station, the steam rising in great white billows that hid the platform where we stood waving good-bye.

CHAPTER 15

Autumn mists and rains drifted over the valleys and hills. Woodsmoke scented the air with a piney fragrance. Obie's house was visible through the bare branches of the pecan trees, but there was never a light in his window.

In November, Franklin Delano Roosevelt was elected to a fourth term as President. Claire wrote articles for the paper about whether women should keep working when the men came home from the war. Seventh grade was keeping me busy and while I missed Obie, I made new friends at school.

At the newspaper office I watched as Claire pasted up a picture, then outlined it with a strip of black tape.

"Is that a V-2 rocket?" I asked. It looked like a small blimp that was kind of hanging over a lady's backyard in London.

"Yes," she replied. "It's filled with fuel and when it hits a building, it explodes. They're really nasty. The Germans are sending them over England, mostly London."

"What about the princesses?" I asked. Since Princess Margaret Rose was about my age I tried to keep track of her.

"I think most of the children have been sent to the country for the duration of the war," Claire replied. "I'm sure both princesses will be safe."

"For your information," I said haughtily, "Princess Margaret Rose is my same age so she's *not* a child."

"You're absolutely right," said Claire, smiling. "I stand corrected."

On the morning we went to cut Christmas trees, the cotton fields were brown and sere, with shreds of cotton clinging to the dead stalks like bits of snow.

Bubba and I helped load the fragrant spruce trees into the back of the truck. Then we threw in bunches of mistletoe that Armistead had shot out of oak trees with his .22 rifle.

We took Miss Clarissa her tree and climbed

back into the truck. "Did you hear her say that Obie's comin' home for the holidays?" I asked.

"Yep," he replied. "I'll be glad to see him."

"Me too," I said, even though I wasn't exactly sure how I felt.

When we got home, Virgie had hot chocolate waiting for us in the kitchen.

"Skates!" said Bubba, finishing his cup. "That's what I want for Christmas. That's all I want and that's what I won't get, I betcha. My pa said that they're scarcer than hen's teeth because of the war. I'll probably get a new bathrobe. Every year I put on my *old* bathrobe to go unwrap my *new* bathrobe. I wish folks wouldn't give you clothes for presents. They don't count."

"I think they do," I said. "I'm hoping for an angora sweater, and I'm going to keep it in the icebox like Claire does so it won't shed."

"That's girl stuff," said Bubba. "I want skates."

"To each his own."

"I wonder what Obie'll be like," he said suddenly, changing the subject.

"I don't know," I replied quietly. "I surely don't know."

On Christmas morning the fields were white with frost and the trees looked black against the pale sky. After breakfast, Armistead drove over to pick up Obie and Miss Clarissa. I was nervous, waiting for them. Finally, there was the rumble of the cattle gap.

Obie looked taller and thinner than when he left. His hair was slicked down with water and parted on the side and he was wearing his usual outfit of starched white shirt and dark trousers. He wore his red sweater and his tie was already out on one side of his collar. Icarus was pressed close to his leg.

"Hey, Tattnall," he said, looking at me hard as if he wasn't real sure it was me. He looked down at his feet in black high-top tennis shoes and up at me again. A smile began slowly, then grew bigger and bigger until his face just beamed.

I found myself smiling back at him.

Obie unwrapped his presents, saving mine until last. I could hardly wait for him to see his new flashlight. The lady at the Yellowfront Store said it had been in the storeroom since before the war, and they had just brought it out and put it in the glass case where I saw it. It was a really nice one. Gently parting the tissue paper, Obie took the flashlight out of the box. Moving his fingers over the smooth handle, he clicked the light on and off several times. He nodded his head and smiled. A moment later, he took the ribbon from the package, and leaning down, tied it slowly and carefully around Icarus's neck. I turned to see if Miss Clarissa had noticed that Obie could tie now, but she was busy unwrapping a present.

When most of the gifts had been opened, Obie handed me a small box. Inside were a piece of petrified wood, so polished and shining that it looked like glass, and a snowy white swan's feather, curled at the tip. It felt cool against my lips.

"I declare," said Miss Clarissa. "I don't know where in the world he finds these things."

I added Obie's gift to the pile of presents I'd received; a pink angora sweater, a Spike Jones record, and a green plaid taffeta dress with a velvet collar.

The telephone rang a few minutes later. It was Bubba.

"Have I got skates!" he said. "Oh, and a new bathrobe. It's plaid and looks like a horse's blanket. And thanks for the compass, Tattnall. It's the second-best present I got. Hey, can you meet me at the courthouse to skate after dinner?"

"Sure," I said, then hung up and joined everyone for dinner. The table practically groaned under the weight of the turkey and all the fixings, plus three desserts: pecan pie, ambrosia, and coconut cake. Everyone ate till they were stuffed.

As I took the last bite of pecan pie, Claire looked over at me.

"Tattnall," she said. "I can't believe it. You had two pieces of pie, two helpings of ambrosia, and enough corn-bread dressing to choke a horse! Keep that up and you won't fit into your angora sweater. You'll look like a fuzzy pink egg."

Obie had eaten steadily through the entire meal. I noticed that he could cut up his meat by himself now. Finally, though, he was finished.

"Bubba wants to try out his new skates and I told him I'd skate with him," I said. "Can somebody please drive me to town after dinner?"

"Sounds like a foregone conclusion to me," said Armistead.

"Sir?"

"Never mind," he said. "I'll take you."

Obie came along, too. On the way, he asked Armistead to stop by his house for a minute. When he came back out, he was carrying a paper bag. "I don't think Icarus can eat any candy," I said to him. "He's stuffed from dinner." Obie kind of ducked his head, like he had a secret.

The downtown streets were deserted. We sat on the bench by the courthouse, putting on our skates and adjusting them with our skate keys. Obie sat next to us, the paper bag in one hand and his flashlight in the other. When we stood up, he reached into the bag and took out a handful of glistening turkey feathers.

"Here," he said. "Put 'em in the backs of your skates. Then you'll fly like wingéd Mercury."

The turkey feathers fluttered as I skated off. Bubba caught up with me and said, "Who the heck is Wing Ed Mercury?"

"Oh, you remember. We read about him in that book of myths. He's the one with wings on his feet."

"Oh, yeah," said Bubba. "I forgot."

The wind held ice in it, and our breath fogged in the crisp air. The sound of our skates rumbled in the still, cold afternoon. Obie and Icarus watched us until late afternoon turned to soft evening, rose-colored clouds glowed on the horizon, and the first stars pricked the heavens. I was glad Obie had come with us. It felt the way things used to be.

Eventually, Bubba's parents drove up and blew the horn. Mr. Tarpley rolled the window down and called, "Let's go, Bubba. We're goin' to your grandma Harper's. Tattnall, you and Obie are welcome to come with us. Mama would be proud to see you."

Zinnia rolled the back window down and yelled, "Hey, Obie, come go with us. She's got goats."

"We can't," I said, skating over to the car. "We'll be goin' home in a minute. Somebody'll be by to pick us up directly. But thank ya'll anyway."

"I didn't ask *you*, Tattnall," Zinnia said.

Bubba smacked her on top of her head as he got in the car. I went over to the driver's seat. "Tell Miz Harper I said Merry Christmas, Mr. Tarpley. Obie does too."

The old car left a trail of exhaust smoke in the dusk. Twilight had fallen and a crescent moon hung clear and golden in a violet sky. I skated around the square, the whirring of my skates the only sound on the still air. When I came around the corner, Obie was standing in the middle of it, waving his new flashlight. He waved the light up and down, up and down; red, green, and gold, it shone in the dusk like a beacon, lighting my way.

CHAPTER 16

The telephone rang right after breakfast. It was Miss Clarissa. She seemed upset.

"Tattnall," she said, "is Obie over there?"

"No, ma'am."

"Are you sure?"

"Yes, ma'am."

"Let me speak to your daddy."

"He's already gone to the paper," I said.

There was a click as she hung up the phone.

I went back to the kitchen, where Virgie was making cheese straws for the New Year's Eve party at our house the next evening.

"She's such a grouch," I said.

"Who?" said Virgie, squeezing gold-colored dough through a pastry tube.

"Miss Clarissa. She didn't believe me that Obie's not over here."

"She's worried 'bout that chile," said Virgie, adding bits of pecans to the straws. "Maybe you ought to go look for him."

"I don't know where he is," I said. "Why am I always supposed to know?" Obie had been back less than a week but it was obvious to everybody that he was unhappy. He'd seemed fine when he first got home. On Christmas Day, when he went with Bubba and me to skate, he'd been like he used to be. But the next afternoon, something happened.

Claire was taking me with her to an afternoon coffee at Ted's parents' house. We were both wearing our angora sweaters and she'd talked Grandmother into letting me wear Tangee lipstick, in a color that was so pale you could barely see it. We'd just come downstairs when Obie came over. He stopped and stared at me as I smacked my lips at the mirror over the fireplace.

"See you later, Obie," Claire said after explaining to him where we were going. "Sorry you can't join us, but it's ladies only," she added gently.

At first Obie didn't say a word. Then he walked up close to me, so close his face was almost touching mine. "You look like a pink egg!" he shouted. Then he stormed off.

I remembered this was what Claire had said to me at Christmas. "You shouldn't have said I looked like an egg," I told her.

"Oh, for pete's sake, Tattnall," she said. "Just get in the car."

Soon after that, Obie started wandering off. Someone'd have to stop what they were doing and go look for him. It was a pain in the neck.

"You'd feel bad if he was lost," said Virgie, putting cookie sheets into the oven.

"He's just off hiding someplace," I said. When she didn't say anything else, I sighed heavily so she'd hear me. But she didn't turn around. "Okay," I said grumpily, "I'll go look."

"Put on a jacket. It's gettin' colder."

"Let's go, Lucky," I said, going out the back door.

The grass was crisp and brown underfoot and the sky was overcast. I walked down the back path and out to the field beyond the house. Lucky raced ahead of me, acting loopy like he always did in cold weather. A minute later, he started barking and Icarus came out of the patch of woods at the edge of the field. The two of them began running around in circles, biting at each other and pretending to fight. I figured Obie couldn't be too far away.

"Obie?" I called. "You out here?"

The wind blew through the pines with a sound like something sighing. I stuck my hands into my pockets to warm them.

"Obie?" I called again. When there was no answer, I headed back to the house. Lying at the edge of the drive was something shiny. It was Obie's flashlight. The glass was broken and the metal dented, as though it had been smashed against a rock, time and again. I reached down to pick it up when suddenly, something hit me between my shoulder blades. The blow caught me off balance and knocked the breath out of me. The ground rushed up to meet me, and for a minute I saw stars. When I tried to breathe, there was an awful pain in my chest. I sat up, trying to catch my breath, and as I did, I saw Obie charging across the lawn.

I was still down on my knees in the grass when Bubba came running over to me.

"You all right?" he asked, panting and out of breath.

"I think so," I said. "What happened?"

"It was Obie!" he said, helping me to my feet. "I was walking up the drive when he came from behind the house. He ran straight at you. I can't believe he did that!"

"Me either," I said, trying to take a deep breath.

"What's wrong with him, anyway?" said Bubba.

"Let's just go inside," I said, brushing the grass off my jeans. "It's gettin' really cold."

In the kitchen, Claire and Virgie were busy covering platters of food with waxed paper and talking to Grandmother as she read from her list of things to do. Bubba put a basket of sausage balls his mama'd made for the party on the kitchen table.

I tried to sneak past Grandmother so she wouldn't ask what had happened to me. But as I walked quickly by, she reached out and put her arm around me. "Why, darlin'," she said, "look at you! Your hair's full of grass . . ." She turned my face toward her. "And the side of your face is all scratched. What happened?"

Everybody turned and looked at me.

"I fell," I said.

She looked over at Bubba, then back at me. "Is somebody going to tell me something?"

"Obie knocked her down," said Bubba.

"What?" said Claire. "When?"

"A little while ago," he said. "Then he ran off somewhere."

"He was only teasing," I said.

A long look passed between Virgie and Claire, then Grandmother walked out of the room. "Now look what you've done," I said to Bubba. "She's gonna call Miss Clarissa."

CHAPTER 17

I didn't tell anybody about finding Obie's flash-light smashed to bits. For some reason, I didn't want them to know. But he must have picked it up himself, 'cause when I went back to look, it was gone, and nobody else mentioned it.

Grandmother's party was a big success. She had been right that everybody needed "cheering up," and they were all eager to throw themselves into the festivities. The war was dragging on and on.

Claire put aside worrying about Ted, who was on board a ship "somewhere in the Pacific." The McIntoshes, who hadn't heard from Michael in a while, but knew that U.S. air raids were taking place over Tokyo, jitterbugged together. And Billy

Malone, whose son was fighting in Germany, was the first to shout "Happy New Year!" ushering in 1945. At the end of the evening, everyone sang "Auld Lang Syne," then left.

After Grandmother had waved good-bye to her guests from the front porch, she came back inside, her deep blue shawl held close.

"It's freezing out!" she said. "Anybody want a last cup of coffee?"

"I'll join you, Mama," said Armistead. He hugged Claire as she started back to the kitchen to help Virgie.

Suddenly Miss Clarissa burst in the door. Her hair was mussed and her coat unbuttoned. "Obie's gone again," she cried. "I took him home after getting him from your place and he went straight to bed. But when I went in to check on him just now, he wasn't there. I don't know where he is."

"I'd better go look for him," said Armistead, putting his coffee cup down.

Grandmother turned to Clarissa. "Take off your coat, darlin', or you'll catch cold when you go back out. Armistead will find him. I'm sure he hasn't gone far. He'll be walkin' in the door any minute now."

But Miss Clarissa wasn't having any of that. "Why would he be walkin' in any minute now,

Mama?" she said. "All he does is run away. He's always running away." She began to cry. "I do the best I can. There's no one to help, to tell me what to do."

"Why, darlin'," said Grandmother, handing her a lacy handkerchief. "We do try to help. You know we're here when you need us."

"It's just not enough," said Miss Clarissa, going over to the fireplace. "I just . . . It's more than I can do!"

Armistead came back into the living room wearing his coat and carrying a flashlight.

"Now, Clarissa," said Grandmother. "Don't take on so." She gave Armistead a look that said, "Do something."

"It's partly *her* fault," said Miss Clarissa, nodding in my direction. "She just abandoned him."

Armistead stopped in his tracks and turned to Miss Clarissa. I could tell from the back of his neck that he was angry.

"Abandoned?" he said. His voice was low but you could hear the anger in it. "No, Clarissa. No one's abandoned anyone. It's not Tattnall's responsibility to do any more for that child than she already has."

Then he came over and put his arm around me. "You go on up to bed now. It's late. We'll find Obie. Don't you worry."

I told everybody good night and went upstairs, but I couldn't fall asleep. I tried pulling the covers over my head, but I couldn't block out the thoughts that whirled around inside it. What Miss Clarissa had said was true, even if Armistead didn't think so.

Armistead found him. He'd heard Icarus barking and he kept walking toward the sound. Obie was down by the pond, holed up in a hunter's deer stand. He was soaking wet and freezing. He'd run and run in his blind flight, then couldn't find his way back in the dark.

The telephone rang just before dawn. Obie was sick. Miss Clarissa had called Dr. Moss, who said that what he had was pneumonia. There wasn't a hospital in Pinella but Dr. Moss came and brought a nurse to help.

Grandmother spent most of her time helping Miss Clarissa. I wasn't allowed to see Obie, no matter how I begged. There were things I wanted to say to him—needed to say to him—but he was too sick to see anybody except the people taking care of him.

CHAPTER 18

In February the ground froze hard enough to strike sparks. The war news continued. General Patton crossed the Rhine River with his troops, and everybody worried about how bitter cold Germany was, and how the men must be suffering. Armistead moved pins on the map: The British offensive had begun in Burma, the Russians were in Warsaw, and the Americans had entered Manila.

Obie was very, very sick. The nurse stayed at his house all the time and he was under an oxygen tent to help him breathe. I still wasn't allowed to see him. At school, for the last half hour of class, Miss Elise would read to us if we hadn't been awful that day. We were in the middle of *The Long Winter* by Laura Ingalls Wilder. I'd already read most of her other books on my own. *The Long Winter* tells how the Ingalls family survived through month after month of blizzards on the prairie, with no trains getting through and hardly any supplies. Life was really hard in those days.

" 'Even after Laura was warm she lay awake listening to the wind's wild tune and thinking of each little house in town, alone in the whirling snow with not even a light from the next house shining through,' " Miss Elise read.

There was a light tap on the door and she looked up from the book. The school secretary came in and handed her a note. Miss Elise read it to herself, closed the book, and came over to my desk. "Tattnall," she said, "will you step out into the hall with me?"

That's when she told me about Obie. I didn't even know I was crying till we got to the office and Miss Elise handed me a tissue. A few minutes later, the school nurse came in. "Your sister's coming to pick you up, darlin'."

Obie was gone. He'd died in his sleep of what Dr. Moss said were "complications" from the pneumonia.

• • •

There is a thing about small towns, a kind of closing in, when something bad happens to one of its own. It's as though everybody forms a circle and keeps the rest of the world outside, the way a mother hen tucks her babies under her wings to protect them. That's the way it was when Obie died.

It seemed like everybody in town stopped by Miss Clarissa's after the funeral. The ladies brought hams, potato salad, fried chicken, vegetables that had been put up the summer before. There were pies, cakes and custards, and whatever other rich dessert the giver was famous for, all offerings from people who wanted to help.

Because it wasn't yet spring, there weren't many flowers in bloom. But what there was had been gathered and brought to the house. Spikes of quince, fragrant narcissus, and early daffodils filled every vase, bringing their light and sweetness to that sad place. People sat in the parlor and spilled over onto the front porch. Most of the men gathered under bare trees, talking to one another, stamping their feet and slapping at their arms like that would keep them warm.

Folks stayed from after the funeral until way into the evening, keeping company with Miss Clarissa so that she wouldn't feel so bad. It didn't seem to do much good, though. She looked like somebody sleepwalking and Virgie said they couldn't get her to eat a mouthful of food.

Bubba, Zinnia, and I sat out on the little screened porch off Miss Clarissa's breakfast room. It was cold, but it seemed better than being inside with so many people.

"I hate it when some lady I don't even know hugs me," I told Bubba. "It doesn't do one particle of good. In fact, it makes me feel worse."

"I know what you mean," said Bubba, "and I already feel about as bad as I can feel."

Virgie came to the door with plates of food for us, then went back inside. Icarus was asleep under Bubba's chair. "You reckon he knows about Obie?" Bubba asked, stroking one of the dog's silky ears.

"I don't know," I said.

"You reckon he's already in heaven with the angels?" Zinnia asked, checking out her plate of food, then looking over at Bubba's to be sure they had equal amounts of everything. She bit into a drumstick.

"Zinnia," Bubba said, "I believe you could eat if the world was comin' to an end."

"Well, *do* you?" she asked, acting like she hadn't even heard him.

"I swear, Zinnia," he said disgustedly. "Sometimes you ask the dumbest questions. Of course Obie's there. It don't take any time a'tall to get to heaven." He tasted a bit of lemon meringue pie.

"You gonna eat your caramel cake?" Zinnia asked, wiping her fingers on her navy corduroy skirt and looking over at my plate.

I passed the cake over to her. "I'm not very hungry."

Bubba stripped the last bit of chicken off the bone and fed it to Icarus.

"Me neither," he said.

"I bet Obie's an angel," said Zinnia. "Do you think so, Tattnall?"

I knew that I was supposed to believe that he was an angel in heaven, but I didn't. I didn't even feel like he was dead.

My mind turned back to the funeral. Our family had sat in the front pew, with me next to Virgie, holding her hand. I hadn't been able to look at the coffin, or even at the flowers that were all over it. The Reverend Allen stood at the pulpit, his black robe gathering the light into its folds. He looked out over the congregation, his eyes dark and kind. Then he looked gently at me.

> "How excellent is thy loving kindness, O God!
> Therefore the children of men put their trust
> Under the shadow of thy wings."

At the organ, Miss Annie Grace began playing "Amazing Grace." As I listened to Obie's favorite hymn, I knew that the only person who should have sung that song was Obie. I thought about the revival when he sang, and of the day in the kitchen when he sang with the mockingbird.

"Well, do you think he's an angel?" Zinnia asked again.

"What?" I said.

"You're not even listening to me," she said. "You act like you're the only one who's sorry Obie's . . . gone."

I looked over at her and saw that she had tears in her eyes.

"I don't know, Zinnia," I said. "I really don't know." I thought about how Obie'd loved to fly, and how he'd loved anything with wings. It seemed to me that he'd always been that way. Even before this past year, when everything went wrong, he'd loved planes and birds, and stories with wings in them. Maybe it was after he got so sick when he was little, and couldn't do a lot of things other kids do, that he'd felt a need for wings. They could lift him up, raise him high so that it didn't matter if he couldn't run fast or play games or swim. Maybe he felt that with wings he could soar above all the things that slowed him down. Maybe he knew that wings could make him free.

With wings, Obie could escape from a world that didn't understand him. I'd understood Obie some, I'd taken care of him as best I could, I'd been his friend. But I hadn't been able to take care of him when he needed me most.

I don't think I'll ever forgive myself for letting Obie down. But I do believe that wherever he is, Obie's forgiven me. There's a hole in my heart because Obie's gone. I'll never forget him.

CHAPTER 19

On a cold March day, I was helping Grandmother in the garden. She planted her sweet-peas on the same day every year. And every year when they bloomed, the ladies would say, "I declare, I don't know how you do it, Margaret." But I knew. It was because she was out grubbing in the dirt, planting those seeds no matter how wet or cold the weather. I'd been trying to help her more and more.

Lucky, who'd been resting near Grandmother's ankle, suddenly got up and loped across the yard. Bubba and Zinnia were coming up the drive, carrying kites.

"Run on," said Grandmother after she'd greeted them. "I'm almost finished here."

I ran inside to get the new box kite that Armistead had brought me from Selma. I hadn't thought much about flying kites lately. I really hadn't had time. The seventh grade was performing *Peter Pan* for the school play and I was Wendy, so most afternoons I had to rehearse till kind of late. But I was glad to see Bubba and Zinnia. We walked down to the cornfield, with Lucky running circles around us.

I'd never flown my kite and it was hard to get it up high. I had to run with it, gradually letting out the string till the wind caught it and lifted the bright yellow box into the blue sky. A few minutes later, I called to Zinnia.

"Hey, I didn't know you liked kites!"

"I don't," she yelled back.

"I told her she couldn't come with me 'less she was gonna fly one," said Bubba, walking up the rise toward me. He was wearing the same old felt hat he'd worn last year when we'd seen the Flying Tigers.

"Seems funny without Obie," he said, looking up at the kites shuddering in the wind.

"Yeah," I said.

Zinnia came over to us. "Is this all there is to it?" she asked.

Bubba gave her a look. "What do you mean?"

She shrugged. "This isn't hard," she said.

"Nobody said it was hard," said Bubba.

"Well, you all acted like flying kites was something special. Like nobody could do it but you all and Obie."

"Aw, get lost, Zinnia," said Bubba. "We never did any such thing."

"Hush a minute," I said. I turned my head, listening.

"What?" said Zinnia.

"Nothing, I guess. For a minute I thought I heard something."

If I closed my eyes, I could pretend that it was last year. That the three kites dancing in the wind belonged to Bubba, Obie, and me. And if I tried hard enough, I could see Obie standing on the rise, listening to the planes long after they had disappeared.

I looked down at the stick that held my kite string, then slowly, so it wouldn't tangle, I let it unwind. My kite began to rise higher than the other two.

"This is for Obie," I said, releasing the last of the string and letting the frail yellow box float away toward the sun.

Bubba dropped his stick, letting the string run out rapidly. "Mine, too," he said.

Zinnia watched as our two kites, released from their tethers, rose into the air. Then, without a word, she let go of her string, and laughed as the three kites soared high into the blue sky.

In April, President Roosevelt died and Harry S. Truman became president of the United States. Then, on May l, there was a special bulletin on the radio: Hitler had committed suicide. Shortly after that, U.S. Armies advanced on Germany and Berlin fell to the Russians.

The whistle began to blow at the fire station; it blew and blew, filling the air with sharp sound. Volunteer firemen rushed to town, but it wasn't a fire.

Armistead stood on the steps of the newspaper office.

"Germany has surrendered!" he shouted.

Then, on August 7, President Harry Truman announced that the atomic bomb had been dropped on Japan the day before. A week later, Japan surrendered. The war was over and September 2, 1945, was set as V-J Day.

Everybody cried and laughed and the telephone nearly rang off the wall. Claire received word that Ted was fine and would be coming home soon. The summer ended, and so had the war.

On an evening in November, Grandmother called up the stairs, "Come quick, Tattnall! Hurry, or you'll miss them!"

Trying not to get run over by Lucky, I went out to the side garden. The sky was the color of sweetbriar roses, and against that tender pink, wild geese flew high in V-formation. Their feathers were gilded by the last of the sun's rays. We watched as the great birds flew away, their haunting calls fading in the twilight.

I thought about Obie and wondered if I'd ever see anything with wings that didn't remind me of him. I knew I'd remember him each time the waxwings returned, and when I heard the sad call of wild geese, and when I felt the cool crispness of a swan's feather.

"Each time I see the birds, I think of our sweet Obie," said Grandmother, taking my hand. "I miss him."

"I miss him, too," I said.